RIKER

SOULLESS KINGS MC

ANDI RHODES

BLUE JOURNEY PUBLISHING

Copyright © 2021 by Andi Rhodes

All rights reserved.

No part of this book may be reproduced in any form or by any electronic or mechanical means, including information storage and retrieval systems, without written permission from the author, except for the use of brief quotations in a book review.

Cover Artwork - © Amanda Walker PA & Design Services

ALSO BY ANDI RHODES

Broken Rebel Brotherhood

Broken Souls

Broken Innocence

Broken Boundaries

Broken Rebel Brotherhood: Complete Series Box set

Broken Rebel Brotherhood: Next Generation

Broken Hearts

Broken Wings

Broken Mind

Bastards and Badges

Stark Revenge

Slade's Fall

Jett's Guard

Soulless Kings MC

Fender

Joker

Piston

Greaser

Riker

Trainwreck

Squirrel

Gibson

Satan's Legacy MC

Snow's Angel

Toga's Demons

Magic's Torment

A NOTE FROM THE AUTHOR:

Riker was written from a very dark place, during the hardest time of my life, and the character's journey reflects that. If you read my books, it's no secret that I like to push the envelope, so to speak. I never shy away from difficult or triggering topics, but I always try to write them with as much grace and accuracy as possible. For Riker and Luna… well, let's just say, things got a bit twisted. The roller coaster these two took me on was a ride unlike any other. It was brutal, gut-wrenching, honest, and very satisfying.

This book contains themes of human trafficking, child abuse (not on the page), sodomy with objects, teen suicide, arson, and extreme violence. If you are someone who is triggered or offended by these things, this book probably isn't for you, and that's okay! But if you don't mind a lot of twists and turns that will ultimately take you to the HEA, I hope you enjoy the ride!

Also, this book is a work of fiction and the product of my imagination and the creative process. The name of the cult at the center of Riker is also fictional. None of the statements in this book are a true reflection of my religious beliefs. I do a

A NOTE FROM THE AUTHOR:

lot of research for every book and this one is no different, but the end result is often embellished and/or manipulated so it fits the story.

While Riker can be read and enjoyed as a standalone, some things carry over from Greaser and Trinity's story. You do not have to read Greaser first, but it will enhance your reading experience.

With all that said, I hope you enjoy Riker and Luna's story. I suggest you grab a box of Kleenex, the nearest bottle of wine or tequila (reader's choice) and buckle up because it's about to get crazy!

Much love,
Andi

PROLOGUE

I can't give in to all the things I would have previously sold my soul to experience.

Luna

Six years ago...

"It's all yours, Luna."

I turn away from the two-sided glass that separates my second-level office from the rest of the club and force a smile at Mollie. She's not only my best friend, but she's also my right-hand woman, the Vice President of the Devil's Handmaidens MC: Oregon chapter. Which is why I'm not decking her where she stands.

"No shit," I snap.

Mollie, or Mousy as the club refers to her, takes a step toward me and reaches out her hand. I sidestep before she can pat my shoulder. I don't like to be touched, at least not when it's coming from a place of pity.

"Look," she begins and holds her hands up as she takes a step back. "I know you didn't want to be made President this way. Hell, none of us expected to lose your mom the way we did. But it happened, Luna. No amount of attitude can put that bullet back in the gun."

"Don't you think I know that?" I grumble and return my attention to the crowd below.

When my mom was murdered a month ago, I inherited the club. And not just the motorcycle club, but the hottest BDSM club in Portland: Jacks and Jills. I grew up straddling both worlds and watching my mom do the same. She was incredible as an MC president, but her true passion came from Jacks and Jills. And when she figured out how to join the two, make them each work to support the other… perfection.

How the fuck am I supposed to live up to that?

"Did you need something else?" I ask Mollie, not bothering to look at her.

I can feel her hovering, and while I appreciate her loyalty, her closeness is making me itch from the inside out.

I can see her reflection in the glass as she shakes her head. "Just wanted to check on you."

"I'm fine."

"Hardly," she scoffs and moves to stand next to me. "Why don't you invite someone up to help take the edge off?"

I shake my head. "I can't."

"Why not?"

"You know why the fuck not."

Mollie sighs and twists to lean her shoulder against the glass. She crosses her arms over her chest and grins at me. "I know why you think you can't," she agrees. "But I also know there isn't a soul in this place who would think any less of you for doing what you need to in order to cope."

I can't stop the snort that escapes. "I can just hear it now." I turn to her. "Badass biker bitch gets her jollies off while grieving the loss of her mother. Oh, and let's not forget all the speculation that would follow about how I'm in no condition to run the Handmaidens or Jacks and Jills." My face falls. "No fucking thanks."

"Hun, you're the only one thinking that." Mollie turns and starts toward the door that leads to the stairwell to the first floor. Before opening it, she glances over her shoulder. "And I suggest you stop before you think it into reality."

I watch as she disappears, and I try to ignore the way her boots thud with each step she takes. The door at the bottom of the stairs slams, rattling the two-way glass I've taken to hiding behind.

I refocus on the crowd below, my gaze zeroing in on the front entrance. Mollie joins Libs at the desk, and I watch as they turn people away.

Jacks and Jills is an exclusive BDSM club and membership is required to enter. The only time membership isn't necessary is on Free for All Days, which only happen once a month. Then and only then can anyone walk in off the street and have a chance to partake in the activities the club provides. Even then, we're selective. We value our members' privacy, and more than a few are powerful people in the Portland community. Typically, on Free for All Days, members stay away, but some aren't able to shut down their desires, even for a night.

You never could.

I shake the thought away because it doesn't matter anymore. Now that I'm in charge, I can't be mingling with members, giving in to the clenching of my pussy every time I see a dom do their thing. I crave being dominated. I crave the vulnerability submitting to a dom gives me. But craving something and being able to have it are two completely separate things.

Movement near the hallway leading to the individual playrooms snags my attention. My eyes fall to the man leaning against the wall, to the woman kneeling in front of him, her head lowered. Fuck, what I wouldn't give to be her right now.

I watch as his lips move, and when she stands, I know he's given her a command. When his fingertips brush against her cheek, push her hair out of the way, he leans in and whispers something in her ear.

Even from this distance, I can see her blush. Hell, I can feel my own as I watch the scene unfold before me. The man wraps his arm around her shoulders and urges her down the hall. As they move farther from view, that's when I see it. This isn't just any man, any dom. No, this man is one I've yet to connect myself to. I've submitted to a lot of doms here at Jacks and Jills, but never him.

I've wanted to though. Dreamt about it. Fantasized about all the ways he'd dominate me, command me into submission. None of that matters anymore though because I can't give in to all the things I would have previously sold my soul to experience. But that was then, and this is now.

Motherfucker!

Why him? Why did I have to see the fucking leather cut, the crowned skull with white and orange rockers? Why the hell did it have to be a Soulless King invading my mind tonight? That has to change and I'm the only one who can make that happen.

All mine?

Not even fucking close.

CHAPTER ONE

I'm going to remind the new management about the badass who came before them.

Riker
Present Day...

"Why the fuck are you still going?"

I swing my cut around my body and shove my arms through to put it on. I took it off when things in the Nightmare Room got bloodier than I expected. Greaser falls behind me as I take the steps two at a time to go up to the main level of the clubhouse.

"Because, I said I would." I shrug. "And I'm a man of my word."

"And the man you made a deal with is dead, brother," Greaser reminds me.

As if I could forget. I was the one who killed David Gorman. The second he took matters into his own hands and entered Trinity's information into a database, he sealed his fate. I have no guilt about taking his life. Like so many, he had to die.

"Dead or not, it doesn't matter."

I enter the code into the keypad, and the steel door swings open into the hallway. I stalk across the wooden floor and out into the main room, toward the bar. Fender and Trainwreck are sitting on stools, both with empty shot glasses in front of them.

"Fender, would you please tell him—"

I whirl on Greaser and grab him by his shirt. His eyes flash fire, and I know they're a reflection of my own anger as well.

"This is none of your fucking business," I snarl as I pull him close. "Leave it alone."

"Aren't you gonna step in, Prez?" Trainwreck's tone holds a bit of sarcasm, which only ratchets up my anger.

"Nah," Fender replies. "Let 'em work it out, whatever the hell *it* is."

Greaser's hands wrap around my wrists. "I don't know why this has you so fucking pissed." He pushes down, and I let my arms fall. "It's my job to protect you and that's all I'm trying to do."

"I don't need protection." I turn around and slide onto the stool next to Fender. "Not from this anyway."

"Okay, I was going to leave you two to go at it, but now I can't," Fender says and lifts his hand to signal to Margo that he wants the shot glasses filled. "G, why does Riker need to be protected?"

A rumble barrels up out of my chest. "I don't."

"Jacks and Jills is off-limits to MCs," Greaser insists. "Has been for almost six years."

A memory enters my mind of the sexy redhead who made that fact very clear the last time I tried to enter the club. I flashed my membership card, and for the first time since I joined, it didn't work.

"We no longer permit motorcycle club members to enter Jacks

and Jills."

"Says who?" I snap, pissed off that this bitch is taking away my ability to ease the ache in my balls.

She crosses her arms, and her cleavage spills over the deep V-neck of her white tee. My eyes drop to stare, and saliva pools under my tongue. I've seen this chick before, many times, but never this close. She's flitted around the club like some submissive whore, taking her pleasure from any dom willing to supply it.

"Says me." She smirks, but it doesn't detract from the way her pupils dilate or her nostrils flare under my scrutiny.

"I wanna see Delia." I shift my gaze to look beyond the redhead toward the second entry door. "Where is she?"

When there is no answer, I return my attention to the chick ruining my night. Her smirk has fallen, and there's something else in her expression, something that has all of my protective instincts kicking in, all of my Dom tendencies.

"What happened to Delia?" I ask, reaching a hand out to tuck it under her chin and lift her gaze to mine.

She shoves my arm away, and any emotion I think I saw disappears as her face hardens. "She's dead."

A bullet to the chest wouldn't have taken me more by surprise. I haven't heard from Delia in a while but... dead? When? How?

And why the fuck didn't I know about this before now?

"Dude, are you even listening?"

I shake my head free of the memory and glance at Fender. "Huh?"

"I was saying I agree with Greaser. Nothing good can come from going to Jacks and Jills."

"Maybe." I shrug. "But I'm a man of my word."

"Yeah, so you keep saying," Greaser mumbles. "Answer me this… how the hell do you plan to get through the door? I'm pretty sure you're on some sort of list after the last time. The kind of list that includes your picture and all the reasons beyond being in an MC that you're banned from the club.

The kind of goddamn list that almost ensures the cops will get called if you show your face."

"I'll never know unless I try."

"Jesus," Fender mutters. "At least take someone with you."

"I'll go," Trainwreck states enthusiastically.

He's a newly patched member, but there are times he acts exactly like the damn kid who walked in the clubhouse declaring he wanted to prospect for the Soulless Kings. Ever since his twin, Trinity, came back into his life, he's changed, hardened, so these glimpses of the old Trainwreck are welcome, if not annoying as hell.

"No," I bark. All eyes turn to me, and I shrug. "I don't need a babysitter."

"Maybe not," Fender agrees. "But keep making shit decisions, and that's gonna change real quick."

"Just leave it the fuck alone," I snap before lifting a newly poured shot and downing it in one quick gulp. I slam the glass down and slide it across the bar top. "Now, if you'll excuse me…"

I turn away from my brothers and stomp toward the door. I shove it open and narrowly miss running into Gibson, the club's doc. When he tries to grab my shirtsleeve to stop me, I shake him free and continue down the steps toward my Harley.

Throwing a leg over the seat, I fire her up. I let the rumble of the machine vibrate into my bones before taking off down the gravel road and leaving the property. A part of me realizes that what I'm about to do is stupid, but I don't let that stop me. I can handle the consequences of stupid. What I can't handle is what happens if I sit back and play it safe. The wondering, the wishing, the *aching*.

Forty-five minutes later, I pull into Jacks and Jills' parking lot and situate my bike in a space as far away from the door as I can. No need to bring attention to myself before I even get to the door.

When I stand to my full height, I take a deep breath. Before I can attempt to get inside, I need to take off my cut, but that's easier said than done. The leather has become a part of me, like a second skin, and taking it off feels disrespectful.

If you want to get through the door, this is what you have to do.

I take the cut off and shove it in my saddle bag. I should have left it at the clubhouse, but if there's one thing a Soulless King never does, it's ride without their colors, unless given permission by their president, and let's face it… Fender was *not* going to allow that.

I glance at the red and blue neon sign that reads 'Jacks and Jills'. The sign looks new, but then again, it's been so long since I've been here, 'new' is a relative term. All I know for sure is it's not the same sign that was here when Delia was in charge.

Delia. Fuck, I miss her.

I shove a hand through my hair and stride toward the door. With each step I take, my thoughts jumble until I'm a giant ball of nerves. My palms sweat, and I wipe them on my jeans before wrapping my hand around the ornate wrought iron door handle and pulling.

When it doesn't budge, I glance around, and my eyes land on a sign next to an intercom system. The sign reads 'Swipe ID for entry'. That's when I notice the card reader to the right of the door.

"Please swipe your ID, sir."

The female voice is staticky as it comes through the intercom system and it's not one I recognize. I don't know if I should be grateful for that or not.

"Sir?" the voice prods.

The intercom is similar to the one we use for the Nightmare Room so I press the button I know will allow me to talk to whoever is on the other side of the door.

"I'm afraid I've lost my ID," I lie.

"That's unfortunate, sir," she says. "You'll have to come back during office hours to apply for a new membership and obtain an ID."

Anger courses through me, setting my veins on fire. I need in this fucking building, and I have no intentions of leaving until I get what I want.

I push the button again. "Can't you make an exception, just this once?" I ask, forcing a careless tone, one I don't feel in the slightest.

"No, sir, an exception can't be made."

"Do you have any fucking—" I press my lips together and inhale deeply before speaking again. "What are the office hours?"

"Those are printed on your welcome packet, sir," the woman informs me and I clench my fists.

"Do you seriously think I know where the hell that is, if I can't even find my ID?" I demand, unable to dampen my rage any longer.

"And do you seriously think I give a damn?" the woman snarls. "I'm just following the fucking rules. I suggest you do the same." There's a long pause, and the speaker crackles. "Now, please leave the premises before I have to call security."

Pain radiates through my fist when it connects with the steel door. I shake out my fingers as if that will make it all better. All the action does is make me more keenly aware of the violence that always flows just beneath the surface, scratching and clawing to be unleashed onto the world. Or at least onto whoever it is who's pissing me off at the moment.

I take a deep breath and press the intercom button.

"For what it's worth, Delia never would have let this shit

fly," I say, not bothering to hide my contempt. "Maybe the bitch in charge should think long and hard about how Jacks and Jills began and how she's driving her mother's legacy into the ground."

I don't stick around to wait for a reply because there's nothing the faceless voice can say to change my mind. When I reach my Harley, I yank open my saddle bag and grab my cut. I put it on and instantly feel more in control, more like myself.

I shove my hand in my back pocket and pull out my wallet. Flipping it open, I look at the two identification cards that always remain front and center: my driver's license and my Jacks and Jills membership ID. My legal name, Dominic Young, taunts me, along with the words under it.

'Platinum Dom' is the designation Delia promoted me to three months after I joined the club. She taught me everything I know about being a dominant, about caring for submissives and myself. And she was proud of that fact, of her ability to share BDSM with others like her.

Her daughter? Not so fucking much.

I take the membership ID out of my wallet and tear it in half, and then I pull my lighter out of my pocket. Flicking the Bic, I touch the flame to the corners of the now ruined ID. A grin spreads across my face as I watch the edges curl and flitter away as ash.

When the card has completely disintegrated, I swing my leg over my Harley and start the engine. I may not have gotten through the door tonight, but I will… soon.

And when I do, I'm going to remind the new management about the badass who came before them, about who I am and why banning me from Jacks and Jills is an unbelievably stupid thing to do.

CHAPTER TWO

We're not in the business of sending girls back to their abuser, no matter who they are.

Luna

"We could really use—"

I flatten my palms on my desk and push myself up, leaning forward on my outstretched arms. My gaze locks with Mollie's, and she tilts her head.

"If you're trying to scare me, save it," she says flippantly. "I'm your VP for a reason and it sure as fuck isn't because I'll cower under your anger."

We stare at each other a few moments longer before she drops into her chair, arms crossed over her chest. Then, and only then, do I straighten. I lift my iPad and scroll through the reported numbers for the night.

"We're at capacity anyway," I say and turn the device so she can see the screen. "Wouldn't wanna get shut down."

"You and I both know we aren't getting shut down." Mollie chuckles. "At least not while the fire chief is a member."

"You've got an answer for everything, don't you?"

She shrugs. "For the most part, yeah."

A knock on the door grabs my attention. "Enter," I call out.

The door swings open, and Libs steps into my office. Her eyes dart from me to Mollie and back again.

"He's gone," Libs tells me.

I glance at the security monitors that show me a view of the parking lot. Something flashes on the black and white screen, and it takes me a moment to realize it's the flame on a lighter.

"You sure about that?" I arch a brow at Libs and tip my head toward the monitor.

"Motherfucker," she mumbles under her breath.

The three of us watch as he takes off out of the lot, in the direction of the coast. When he first arrived, he took his cut off, and I still couldn't make out the patches when he put it back on. But I know exactly what it looks like. The crowned skull and enforcer patch have haunted my dreams, taken over my fantasies for years.

I flop down in my chair. "How is everything else going downstairs?" I ask Libs.

"Business as usual," she says.

"You'd know that if you went down," Mollie says through tight lips.

I brace myself for the same argument Mollie and the rest of the club have given me for the last six years. I don't know why they bother. It hasn't worked up to this point and it's not going to work. I do what I do, or don't do, for a reason.

Mollie and Libs don't disappoint. They're nothing if not consistent… or maybe insistent is a better word. Fortunately, I perfected the art of tuning them out. I had to, otherwise, I'll do something I'll regret. And I've spent six years ensuring I have no regrets.

"You two can stop," I snap when they keep droning on about all the ways sex would benefit me.

"I just don't understand," Libs whines, and I have to stop myself from cringing at the sound. "What harm could it do to fuck someone?"

"You're both dismissed."

Mollie's eyes widen, while Libs' face falls. It's clear by their expressions they want to stay right where they are and argue, but they both wisely choose to stand and leave my office.

When I'm alone, my gaze seeks out the security monitors again. Everything looks normal. Why, then, is there a ball of dread forming in my gut?

I pick up my iPad and tap on the icon for the software we had developed to serve as a virtual waiting room for our private scene rooms. Not only are the rooms all full, but there are also members signed up to use them when they become available. Business is booming.

My cell vibrates in my pocket, startling me out of my concentration. I pull it out and swipe up to read the new text.

Mollie: We have a problem.

My muscles tense as I stand and move to the massive window overlooking the main floor. My eyes land on Mollie, who's standing at the end of the bar, looking up at me. As if she can feel my stare, she tips her head toward the entrance. When I glance in that direction, the rage that's constantly simmering just beneath the surface explodes.

What the fuck?

As I stride across the room, I punch out a quick text to my Devil's Handmaidens MC sisters.

Me: Code black.

I quickly descend the steps and weave my way through the crowd. The smell of whiskey invades my senses when I bump into a member and his drink sloshes over the glass and onto my skin. I shake the liquid off and keep walking. Before I make it to the entrance, Mollie, Libs, and four other sisters are flanking me.

We reach the door and circle around the girl—because like all the others, she is just a girl—who triggered the code black. Her eyes dart from one member to another, and fear is etched into her expression. I wrap my arm around her shoulders and ignore the way she cowers under me. Fear is typically something I strive to induce, but when it's coming from a victim, it infuriates me.

"You're safe," I say as I pull her close. "I promise."

I've said those four words countless times over the last six years, yet they still feel like a lie. I can't promise safety… I can't promise shit. But that hasn't stopped me from trying.

"What's your name, Hun?" I ask the girl.

While I wait for her to respond, I guide her toward the steps that lead upstairs to my office. Other than my DHMC sisters, victims are the only people permitted beyond the door at the bottom of the stairwell.

"Paulina," she responds as I punch in the passcode to open the door.

"Paulina," I repeat. "That's a pretty name. I'm Luna." She nods and looks at the other woman surrounding us. I introduce her to them one by one. "That's Mollie and Libs. Then you've got Pivot and Stormy, Spooks and Lashes."

"Nice to meet you," Paulina mumbles.

"How old are you?" Pivot asks, not bothering to hide her disdain.

Paulina's eyes dart to me then back to Pivot. "I, um, nineteen."

"Bullshit," Pivot counters, and I shoot her a glare. She

shrugs. "What? She can't be more than fifteen and that's being generous."

"Maybe," I concede. "But that only makes it worse, and you know it."

"Never said otherwise."

I take a deep breath, wishing this wasn't my life, wishing things could go back to the way they were before murder and mayhem rocked my world.

"Get back to the floor, all of you," I demand. "I've got it from here."

They do as they're told, and when it's just Paulina and me, I urge her the rest of the way upstairs. Her shoulders remain tense, but that's to be expected. I don't know how she found us, nor do I care. She's here and that's all that matters.

I guide her to a chair and press her into it. Surprisingly, she doesn't resist. I busy myself with getting her a drink and something to eat. If I've learned anything over the years, it's that when girls show up here, they've usually been running for days with little to no food.

"Here."

I thrust a Coke at her, along with a peanut butter and jelly sandwich. She stares at the offerings for a long second before taking both and devouring them. When she's done, she sets the empty can on the desk and folds her hands in her lap.

"So, Paulina," I begin as I sit across from her. "Was Pivot right about your age?"

She shrugs. "Does it matter?"

My lips tilt into a grin. This girl may have been beaten down and trafficked, but there's still a bit of backbone in there.

"Yes and no." I lean back in my chair and cross my arms over my chest. "I don't give a damn if you're a minor, other than it fuels my rage at whoever sent you running, but I do care about whether or not you're being honest with me."

A wrinkle appears across her forehead. "I'm sixteen."

I nod, as if knowing the truth somehow makes the situation better. It doesn't.

"Is there anyone who will come looking for you?"

The question is pointless. Of course someone will come looking for her. There's always someone looking. The true question is whether or not the people looking are good or evil, friend or foe.

Paulina brushes her hair out of her face. "Maybe."

I arch a brow at her, waiting for her to elaborate, but she doesn't. "You don't know?"

"My dad might come for me," she says before pulling her bottom lip between her teeth.

Something in her tone makes the hairs on the back of my neck stand up. Most girls in her situation would be happy to have family looking for them, but she's not.

Why?

"What's your dad's name?" I ask, dreading the answer.

"If I tell you, you'll send me away." Panic infuses her tone, which puts me on high alert.

"No, I won't." I lean forward, resting my elbows on the desk. "We're not in the business of sending girls back to their abuser, no matter who they are."

"His name is Conrad." My stomach drops to the floor. "Conrad Templeton."

What. The. Actual. Fuck?

CHAPTER THREE

The club's way isn't always the best way or the only way. But it is the accepted way.

Riker

"Can I get you another?"

I draw on the cigarette between my lips and push the whiskey glass across the bar. The bartender pours the liquor, but when I point to the glass, she adds more.

"Aiming for comfortably numb or obliterated?"

"I'm aiming for some peace and quiet," I snap without looking at her. "If I wanted to play twenty questions, I'd have gone home."

"Asshole," she mumbles under her breath before moving down to the other end of the bar to take care of other customers.

When I left Jacks and Jills, I rode around for a while before settling at a bar halfway between there and the clubhouse. There were no other bikes in the parking lot, which suited me just fine. I'm in no mood to get into a turf war, but

I wouldn't shy away from one either. And in my current state, it'd end bloody.

"This seat taken?"

I twist and my eyes lock onto a pair of baby blues that would normally pierce straight to my cock. Without responding, I return to face forward and stab my cigarette out in the ashtray. The woman slides onto the stool next to me and lifts her fingers to snag the bartender's attention.

"What'll it be?" the bartender asks.

"Gin and tonic. Oh, and put it on his tab."

The bartender quickly glances at me before returning her attention back to the woman. "Uh, you sure about that?"

"It's fine," I say.

I lift my glass to my lips and down the contents. After slamming the tumbler down, I pull out my wallet and toss three twenties onto the bar. I walk to the exit and shove the door open to step out into the cool night air.

The wind has picked up since I arrived, so I put my head down and shove my hands into my pockets. My boots thud across the pavement as I stride to my Harley.

"I'm a little disappointed."

I whip my head up and see Trainwreck standing next to his own bike, which is parked in front of mine.

"What the fuck are you doing here?" I bark, annoyed that he's here and pissed off that I didn't notice him the second I stepped outside.

"I could ask you the same thing," he quips.

I narrow my eyes at him and watch as he reaches into his pocket. When he pulls out a joint, I yank it from his fingers and stick it between my lips.

"Thanks," I say around the paper.

I flick my lighter and touch it to the tip, inhaling deeply to get the flame to catch. I blow out a cloud of smoke and feel the drug curl around my insides.

"Now, answer my question," I demand and pass the joint to him. "Why the fuck are you here? Did one of the brothers send you to babysit me?"

"Nah, nothing like that." Trainwreck takes a hit. "I wanted to talk to you about something though."

"And you had to stalk me to do it?"

"No." He shrugs. "But I didn't think it was something that I should bring up at the clubhouse… at least not yet."

"Shit, is there another sister we don't know about?"

Trainwreck slugs me in the arm, and damn if it doesn't hurt. He's packed on the muscle in the last few months.

"Ha ha, very funny." Trainwreck pulls his cell phone out of his cut and taps on the screen until he finds whatever he's looking for. He flips it around so I can look at it. "He look familiar to you?"

The man in the picture is short and bald, but he's dressed in a tux. The watch on his wrist probably cost him more than my Harley, and he's smiling at the camera. He has his arms around two young girls, who are standing on either side of him.

"Should he?"

Trainwreck taps the screen a few more times before turning it back toward me. I glance at it and see he's pulled up a news article with the headline *Billionaire's Daughter Disappears.* The date on the article is two days ago.

"Okay, so what? He ask for the club's help finding his daughter or something?"

"The guy's name is Conrad Templeton." Trainwreck rocks back on his heels. "And I'm pretty sure he's the leader of whatever sick game Trinity's kidnappers were playing."

Unease pricks my skin.

"Please tell me you've taken this information to Fender or Greaser or your sister… hell, anyone other than me." He shakes his head. "Why the fuck not?"

"Because, Riker, you know as well as I do, if I take this to the club, a plan will be made and executed to take this guy out. Not to mention, Trinity and Greaser don't need the stress right now. Trenton is only a few months old, and their focus needs to be on their son."

"What's wrong with that? We do things the way we do them for a reason."

"I know. But if we go straight to the leader, what happens to all the others in the game? Templeton disappears and someone else is only going to take over. We need to work from the bottom up."

I let his words bounce around in my brain. They make sense. *He* makes sense. And that pisses me off because it makes me realize that the club's way isn't always the best way or the only way. But it *is* the accepted way.

Wrapping a hand around my neck, I try to think of how to tell him he's right without inflating his ego.

"C'mon, man," he urges.

"Let's say I agree with you," I begin and glare when he grins. "What am I supposed to do with this information?"

"I don't know," Trainwreck admits. "But I think finding the daughter is the key to this whole thing."

"You know I have to take this to church, right?"

"But I—"

"But nothing," I snap. "I understand why you brought it to me, but at the end of the day, that's not how the Soulless Kings roll, and you fucking know it."

"What if th—"

"Stop!" I shout. "I don't deal in what ifs, and neither should you. We'll both take it to church, and whatever the club decides, that's what we do."

"If I wanted to do what the club decides, I'd—"

Trainwreck's head whips to the side after my fist connects with his jaw. His eyes widen, and he spits out blood.

"What the hell was that for?" he asks as he grips his jaw and wiggles it from side to side as if testing to see whether or not it's broken.

"I get it, you've had a rough go of things lately, what with your sister coming back from the dead and shit, but that doesn't give you license to do whatever the fuck you want with no regard for the Soulless Kings." I take a deep breath and narrow my eyes. "You've only been a patched member for a short time, and you're one of the best we've got. But don't for a second think it can't all be taken away in a heartbeat, because it can." I snap my fingers. "Just like that, everything you know, everyone you love… gone. All because you let your emotions dictate your actions." I take a step toward my bike and throw my leg over the seat. "Now, I'm heading home. I suggest you follow."

I fire up my Harley and tear out of the parking lot. When I reach the end of the block and stop at the stop sign, I hear the rumble of his bike. Glancing over my shoulder, I see he's taking my advice.

When he pulls up beside me, I reach out to fist bump him. It takes Trainwreck a second, but he knocks his knuckles with mine. That's the thing about being a Soulless King… we're quick to anger, to fire off at the mouth, but through it all, we're brothers. We're family and that remains at the core of everything we do.

CHAPTER FOUR

The world isn't goddamn perfect.

Luna

The ax bounces off the wooden target and falls to the ground. I shake my arms out, as if they're the problem, before lifting another ax to throw. Just as the weapon leaves my grasp to sail through the air, the sound of twigs snapping reaches my ears.

"If I wanted company, I'd have asked for it," I call out.

I turn and see Spooks stepping out from between the trees and under the motion lights we put out here, a flask in one hand and a bottle of water in another. Her jet-black hair is streaked with silver and pulled into a ponytail at the top of her head.

"Figured you could use a break," she says and thrusts the water at me. "You've been out here for hours."

I take the bottle of water and drink greedily from it. When I put the cap back on and toss the plastic to the ground, I nod toward the flask. "Isn't it a little early for alcohol?"

Spooks is right about one thing… I've been out here for hours. In fact, when we returned from the safe house around three in the morning, I never went inside. So, it is way too fucking early for the liquor to be flowing.

Spooks shrugs. "Eh, it's just a little hair of the dog."

"In other words, it's that homemade moonshine shit you all insist on drinking."

"Yep."

She takes another sip from the flask before screwing the cap back on and shoving it in her back pocket.

"So, what's got your panties in a wad?"

That's Spooks for you. When she's not lurking in the shadows and, well, spooking people, she fancies herself a goddamn comedian.

"Nothing."

I lift another ax and launch it at the target. This time, it sticks. Spooks steps next to me and throws one. When it also sticks, my blood simmers. I'm the best ax thrower in the club, and the fact that she got it to stick on her first try of the day doesn't sit well with me.

"If it was nothing," she begins. "I'd be dragging your ass outta bed, not outta the woods."

"Any updates from the safe house?" I ask, in an effort to change the subject.

"No." Spooks heaves a sigh. "But you knew that."

I walk toward the target to retrieve all of the axes. I fill my hands with as many as I can and return to my spot by the bench. The entire time, I keep reminding myself why I can't use one of the axes on Spooks.

She's a sister.
She means well.
Murder is bad.

Okay, that last one doesn't really apply. I've killed plenty of people, all who deserved to die because of their sins. But Spooks doesn't fall into that category. Annoying as hell? Absofuckinglutely. But a sinner who's earned my wrath? Not so much.

A Devil's Handmaiden doesn't murder for no reason. The average person is safe from us, from me.

"Are the others awake? Or are you the only one stupid enough to crawl out of bed and come annoy the fuck out of me?"

Spooks grins and I have to force myself not to smack the attitude off her face.

"I prefer to think of it as having a set of brass knockers," she quips as she cups her tits and pushes them up.

Always a fucking comedian.

"Still doesn't answer my question."

She drops her arms and rolls her eyes. "Mollie was in the shower when I left the clubhouse, and Pivot was eating her usual breakfast. The rest were still in bed."

Bed. A few hours of sleep sounds heavenly right about now, but my responsibilities as president come first.

"Head on back and tell them we're meeting in an hour."

"And I should tell them we're meeting about…"

"Does it matter?" I arch a brow at her.

"Nope." Spooks starts walking backward, and before turning around to disappear into the trees, she says, "But can you at least shower before we meet? You fucking stink."

I throw an ax in her direction, and it whizzes by her head. The sound of her laughing fills the air.

"Fucking bitch," I mumble under my breath and plop down on the bench.

I thrust shaky fingers through my hair. I should head to the clubhouse and eat something, but how am I supposed to do that? How am I supposed to do normal things with what's going on?

You just do.

And with that in mind, I stand and walk through the woods toward the clubhouse, toward home. I put one foot in front of the other and just do it.

∽

"If I'm understanding this right, we have Conrad Templeton's daughter at one of our safe houses?"

I nod at Lashes. "She was our code black."

"And you're just now telling us this?" Lashes fiddles with the strip of leather she always carries. "Don't you think this is something we should have known right away?"

"Maybe," I concede, hostility in my tone. "But I had to digest the info first."

"Am I missing something?" Pivot asks.

Pivot joined Devil's Handmaidens MC five years ago and quickly worked up the ranks to become our Enforcer. She's smart, beautiful, and a genius with her spikes. She's also quick to anger and will turn on someone quicker than they could blink.

When no one answers her, Pivot shifts her eyes from one member to another.

"Would someone just spit it the fuck out?" she snaps. "Who the hell is Conr—"

"He killed Delia," Mollie says quietly. When I glare at her, she doesn't make eye contact.

"Wait," Pivot stands from her chair and flattens her palms on the table to brace herself. "Delia? As in your mother, previous club president?" she asks and locks her eyes on mine.

"One and the same," I say with a hint of snark in my tone.

"He's also the leader of a religious cult that runs the largest human trafficking ring in the country… and I use the term 'religious' lightly."

"If you know he's the one who killed your mom, why is he still breathing?"

A wave of fury crashes over me, making it difficult to breathe. It's not Pivot's fault I'm angry. I don't talk about my mom's murder much, instead focusing my efforts, the *club's* efforts, on being a safe haven for escaped victims of human trafficking.

I close my eyes and inhale slowly through my nose, counting to ten as I do. I hold the air in my lungs until the room starts to spin and then force the air out through my mouth.

When I open my eyes, everyone is staring at me. "What?"

They all shake their heads or avert their gazes. I take another deep breath, this time trying to bolster myself before continuing to discuss Templeton and the pure evil he brings to the world.

"Pivot, to answer your question, he's still breathing because we haven't been able to track him down."

"Not for lack of trying," Mollie adds hotly. "Going after him is like playing a game of whack-a-mole. I've never seen someone who is so out in the open at public events and also impossible to actually get near in person. Every time we think we're close, we come up against another one of his Soldiers of Sin. As the messiah, or *Lord Luxuria* as he calls himself, he's protected."

"Lord Luxuria?" Pivot questions.

"Yeah," I deadpan. "Luxuria is one of the seven deadly sins… lust, fornication."

"Nice guy," Pivot mumbles.

"Google him sometime," I tell her. "There's plenty of information available. At least as far as who he is in the eyes of the general public." I sweep my gaze around the room. "Anyway, his daughter, Paulina, escaped and was our code black. We need to figure out how to use this to our advantage."

"It's simple," Libs states. "We use the daughter as bait."

"No fucking way," I bark. "We've worked too hard to become a safe place for victims, and I'm not going to screw that up by turning the tables on them."

"I'll probably get desk duty for this," Spooks says. "But what about asking—"

"You're right," I snap. "You've got desk duty for a week. No playtime at Jacks and Jills."

"C'mon, Looney Tunes," Mollie cajoles. "You know he could help. Not to mention how much stronger we'd be with the Soulless Kings at our back."

I grind my teeth at her use of my road name. *Looney Tunes.* I earned the name because, according to them, I can be batshit crazy. And if I'm being honest, I love it. It fits. But when Mollie uses it in that tone, the one that screams 'you're not being rational', it pisses me right the fuck off.

"No!" I shout as I bang my fists on the table, savoring the pain that vibrates through my hand and up my arms. "We can handle this on our own."

To me, my words sound hollow, forced, and stupid as hell. We've been trying to do this on our own since the night I found my mom lying in a pool of her own blood on the floor at Jacks and Jills. We've been trying, and we've been failing… over and over and over again.

"Then what do you suggest?" Stormy asks.

Stormy has been quiet since the meeting began, intensely taking in every single word. That's her way. Half the time you could forget she's even there. Like a hurricane brewing in the ocean, you don't feel her wrath until she wants you to.

But when she decides to show you, you better batten down the hatches.

I shove the image of my dead mother out of my head. "The first thing we need to do is talk to Paulina, get as much information as we can from her. We can't afford to rush things, not if we want an actual shot at taking Templeton out."

"That's not exactly a solid plan," Spooks points out.

"Maybe not, but it's all we've got… for now."

"All in favor, raise your hand," Mollie calls out for a vote.

Spooks is the only one who doesn't lift her hand, but when she notices she's alone in her vote, she gives in.

"I want it noted that I'm only agreeing because I don't want any more than the one week of desk duty. One week with no sex is enough."

"It's not that bad," I say, thinking of my own stint with celibacy.

"Not everyone is built like you and can go without cock for years on end," Spooks says around a laugh. "My pussy would hate me."

I ignore her words. "I'll be heading to the safe house later today, to talk with Paulina. Mollie, Stormy, and Pivot, you're with me." I turn to the other three in the room. "Lashes, Spooks, and Libs, you need to head to the club and get ready for tonight. The club is booked for a member's birthday and he's one of the longest members we've had. We can't fuck the party up."

Once everyone agrees with their assignments, I end the meeting. Mollie stays behind after the others file out of the room.

"What?" I ask warily.

"Are you really not going to call him?"

"Are you really asking me that?" I counter.

Mollie sighs and shrugs.

"Look, he wasn't there six years ago when he was supposed to be. If he had been, my mom would still be here. And there's nothing to indicate to me that things would be different now."

"Yeah, Looney Tunes, he wasn't," Mollie agrees before taking a deep breath. "But ne—"

"Don't." I turn away from her, toward a window that overlooks the property, as my breath catches in my throat and my eyes begin to burn. "Don't say it."

"Neither were you."

Tears spill down my cheeks. She said it. She fucking said the one thing that she knows can break me. This is one of those times I wish she'd embrace her road name and be a little more mousy, quieter, unassuming.

Her boots thud on the hardwood as she leaves the room. I swipe the wetness from my face and stare at the trees, wishing things were different.

In a perfect world, my mom would be standing next to me, talking about her latest idea to make Jacks and Jills better or how beautiful the sunrise was to watch on the back of her bike. In a perfect world, *he* wouldn't exist. In a perfect world, I wouldn't have been exploring my submissive side with some random dom in his basement scene room six years ago.

Unfortunately, the world isn't goddamn perfect.

CHAPTER FIVE

Why then, does the thought of saying I'm sorry to her fill me with dread?

Riker

"Shut the fuck up so we can get started."

Voices lower and eyes turn to Fender. He wasn't happy when I asked him to call church, and his tone makes his anger clear.

"Riker," he says, facing me. "Does Trainwreck need to be in here now or do you want to give us the rundown of what the hell is going on first?"

For a brief moment, I contemplate putting all of this off on Trainwreck, but just as quickly, I dismiss the idea. Sure, it's his information I'm sharing, but I'm the senior patched member.

I rise from my chair. "I'll start."

I look around the table, locking eyes for a second with each of my brothers, and stopping when I get to Greaser. "Trainwreck thinks he found the leader of the game that got Trinity kidnapped."

"What the fuck?!" Greaser shouts. He stands so fast his chair crashes to the floor. "Why wouldn't he—"

"Sit. Down." Fender orders.

Greaser glares at him for a long moment before finally complying. "This is bullshit. Why would he go to Riker about this?"

"I don't know," Fender responds. "But we're not going to get that answer if you explode like that."

"Greaser, he came to me because he wasn't even sure if the information he got was accurate." I even out my tone. "Besides, with Trenton, he didn't want to add more shit to yours and Trinity's plates."

At the mention of his son, Greaser calms slightly. "And what information is that?"

I grab Squirrel's laptop from him and type a few keywords into the search bar of the internet browser. When the article I want pops up, I click on it and sync the laptop with the projector.

"Why do we care about some rich bitch who disappeared?" Greaser asks.

"We care because her daddy is Conrad Templeton."

Silence settles over the room as my brothers exchange confused looks.

"I've heard of him," Squirrel finally says. "He's filthy rich, attends some pretty fancy charity events, always willing to give an interview. Basically, he's a prick who wants people to see him as someone he's not."

"Okay, but why does Trainwreck think he's the leader or whatever?" Greaser prods, his face red from pent-up anger.

"Apparently, our newest Soulless King has been doing a lot of digging and research since Trinity showed up."

"On his own?" Fender demands.

I nod as I wrap my hand around my neck. "Anyway, I've

looked through some of it and while I'm not convinced he's right, I do think it's worth digging a little deeper."

Squirrel drags his laptop toward him, and his fingers fly over the keys. Within seconds, the image on the projector screen changes.

"What are we looking at?" I ask.

"That's a list of all the known aliases of Conrad Templeton, as well as bank accounts, travel records, family members." Squirrel grins. "In short, it's proof that Conrad Templeton isn't who he wants the public to believe he is."

"How the hell did you do that so fast?"

"It's what I do." Squirrel shrugs. "I'm damn good, too."

It's not like Squirrel's abilities are new to any of us, but every time he shows off his skills, I'm amazed. I can type shit into Google, but what he just did? No fucking way.

I read one of the aliases out loud. "Lord Luxuria. What the fuck?"

Squirrel's fingers work some more, and a new website pops up on the screen.

"Soldiers of Sin, Lord Luxuria, Church of Sinfinite Opportunity... what the hell is this?" Fender asks, his eyes narrowed at the screen.

"Looks like some sort of cult," I say, my mind whirling.

Squirrel scrolls through the website, and when the bottom of the site comes into view on the screen, my stomach drops.

"There you go," Greaser says and walks to the screen. He taps the bottom. "Right there, in black and white... Picky Daters."

The font is small and part of the fine print that no one ever reads. But it does link Conrad Templeton to Trinity's kidnappers.

"Remember what Dr. Masters told Trinity in the Nightmare Room?" Greaser adds. "About being matched with traffickers on Picky Daters on the dark web?"

"So this guy is a criminal mastermind who wants his followers to believe he's some sort of messiah," Joker says. "And then links his human trafficking site to his cult site. He's either very stupid or an insanely cocky motherfucker."

"Based on all of this, I'd say insanely cocky motherfucker is an accurate description."

"Get Trainwreck in here," Fender commands me.

I walk to the door and when I open it, Trainwreck is there, leaning against the frame.

"Jesus," I mutter, startled.

"How's it going in there?" he asks.

"We're ready for you."

I turn to walk back toward the center of the room, leaving Trainwreck to follow. The click of the door closing reaches my ears, along with the thud of him dropping his weapon in the designated box by the door.

"So, what's the plan?" Trainwreck asks as he steps next to me.

Fender closes the distance between him and Trainwreck. He wraps his fingers around the newest patched member's throat before pushing him backward toward the wall and slamming him against it.

"If you ever pull this shit again, I'll cut that patch off your cut myself," Fender snarls. "Got it?"

Trainwreck narrows his eyes, unphased by the threat. He knows he crossed a line when he didn't go straight to the club as a whole with his information. Not to mention all the digging he did on his own. Not only could he have gotten himself hurt, but he could have brought more than a little trouble to our doorstep.

"Got it."

"Soulless Kings don't act alone."

"Yeah, Prez, I get it," Trainwreck assures him.

Fender drops his arm and walks back to the head of the table. "Anyone else have anything to say to Trainwreck about his actions?"

"I do," Greaser says and Fender nods to give him permission. Greaser turns to face Trainwreck. "You should have come to me. Not Riker, but me. I'm married to your sister, we have a son…" Greaser shakes his head. "You should've fucking come to me."

Greaser drops into his chair and crosses his arms over his chest. Not only is he angry, he's hurt.

"Look, guys," Trainwreck begins and slowly walks toward the rest of us. "I'm sorry, okay?" He hangs his head. "In my own way, I was only trying to protect everyone."

"We don't need your protection," I grit out. "We're a team, a family. We work together, not alone."

"Let's move on," Joker adds to the conversation. "Trainwreck knows he fucked up, and he knows the consequences if he does it again."

"Agreed." Fender's shoulders relax slightly. "Trainwreck, fill us in on what you know."

Trainwreck explains what he told me in the parking lot last night, which is pretty much what I already said.

"Your information is solid," I tell him as I point to the projector screen. "Conrad Templeton is an evil fucker. Now we need to take him down."

Trainwreck nods slowly. "I know, but…"

"But what, Trainwreck?" Fender prods.

"The guy needs to die, there's no denying that." Trainwreck moves to stand next to the screen and taps it. "And we'll make sure that happens. But I think we need to go at this a bit differently than we usually do."

"How so?"

"We can't go straight to him." Trainwreck grins. "We need

to take out the whole fucking organization. Start from the bottom up so there's no one left to fill his shoes."

"I don't disagree with that," Greaser states. "But there are always gonna be sick fucks in the world. No matter who we take out first, there will be more to take out later."

I turn my attention to Fender in an effort to gauge his reaction because it'll be his call how we proceed. We'll vote, sure, but he has the power to veto that if he so chooses. And if the tension in his shoulders or the respect in his expression are any indication, this isn't going to go how Trainwreck feared.

"I'm with Trainwreck," Fender says. "I think we should follow his lead."

Greaser whips his head in our Prez's direction, his eyes narrowed. "You've got to be kidding me!" he shouts. "He's a fucking MC newbie, practically a baby in this life. You can't really think letting him run the show is the right choice?"

"I didn't say anything about letting him run the show," Fender snarls and glares at Greaser. "But even you have to admit he's got a point. Take your emotions out of the equation, G, and think about it. If we start from the bottom and work our way up, we're ridding the world of a lot of fucking evil. If we focus only on the head of the snake, are we really accomplishing anything other than revenge?"

"Revenge is pretty damn sweet," I add. "We've all done things to get revenge and it feels pretty fucking good."

"Of course it is," Fender agrees. "But this isn't about revenge, is it?"

"No, it's not," Trainwreck says. All eyes turn to him. "Do I want Templeton to die? Yes, I believe I've already established that. But more than that, I don't want anyone else to suffer at the hands of these assholes the way Trinity did."

"Let's put it to a vote and see where we stand," Fender

states. "All in favor of working from the bottom up, thump twice."

Greaser is the only one who doesn't vote in favor of that plan.

"Sorry, G, but majority wins." Fender gives Greaser a sympathetic smile, but it's brief. Then, he turns to me. "Riker, I want you and Trainwreck to sit down and strategize. Once you have a solid plan of attack, call church." He turns to Squirrel. "You need to work with them. You're the only one who can dig for info as quickly as we need it. Your skills can help facilitate a plan that will work."

"Sure thing, Prez," Squirrel says.

"As for the rest of you," Fender begins. "Be ready to meet at a moment's notice. And remember, what's said in church stays in church. I don't want any of the ol' ladies catching wind of this. No need to worry them before it's necessary."

Joker bangs the gavel. "Church is adjourned."

Patched members file out of the room until Fender and I are the only two remaining.

"Was there something else you wanted to talk about?" Fender asks.

I flex my fists at my sides. "It didn't go well at Jacks and Jills," I admit.

"Didn't think it would."

"Prez, I need to let off some steam." I avert my gaze for a moment before locking eyes with him. "Got anything for me?"

"Riker, you know there are no side projects in the Soulless Kings." Fender claps me on the back. "I can't just give you a name, an address, and my blessing to go be violent because you need it."

"Yeah, I know." I force a grin. "It was worth a try."

"If you need to let off steam that bad, go back to Jacks and Jills and try again."

"What? Now you're on board with it?" I ask. "Because you've been against me spending time there for as long as I can remember."

"I'm not against the club, bro. I'm against you doing anything that can ultimately end up hurting you. Obviously, it's hurting you more not to be there. So," he shrugs. "Try again."

With those words, he exits the room, letting the door close behind him.

Can I do that? Can I just go back to Jacks and Jills and try again? What would that even look like?

It might go better if you apologize first.

A groan escapes past my lips. Apologize. For some people, that might be easy. It's only two words… three syllables.

I'm sorry.

See, it's not so bad.

Why then, does the thought of saying that phrase to *her* fill me with dread?

CHAPTER SIX

Well, fuck.

Luna

"She hasn't come out of the bathroom in hours. I did hear the shower, and I set clean clothes outside the door for her. They're gone so I know she took them."

I smile at Barb before swiveling my head to glance down the hallway toward one of the bathrooms in the safe house. The tension when I arrived was palpable, rolling off the resident's bodies in waves. It reminded me of the way heat seems to ripple in the air on a hot summer day. It's stifling.

I take in the way the girls are hunched in on themselves on the couch, refusing to make eye contact with me. I see the way they track my every move while trying not to be obvious. I see it, and I hate it.

I nod at Mollie, Stormy, and Pivot, who are all standing just inside the door. They're here to handle this issue so I can deal with our newest arrival.

"Thanks, Barb."

I pat Barb on the shoulder as I pass her to walk to the bathroom. She doesn't flinch, which is a huge improvement from the night she showed up at Jacks and Jills three years ago, covered in bruises and full of fear. Barb was a unique case in that her family didn't want her back. They were loyal members of The Church of Sinfinite Opportunity... still are. So Barb stayed and has become a sort of den mother to victims as they show up, at least for this safe house.

When I reach the bathroom door, I press my ear to the wood. No noise comes from inside, but I can see the light under the door, as well as the shadow of someone moving around.

"Paulina," I call softly as I knock.

No answer.

"Hun, is everything okay?"

Again, no answer.

I turn and lean my back against the wooden barrier. "You don't have to talk if you don't want to," I tell her. "But I'm going to, so I need you to listen, okay?"

Silence.

"Do you have any idea how brave you are for escaping?" I ask, knowing she's not going to respond. "So fucking brave. I know you're scared, and this is all probably very overwhelming, but you're not alone." I turn around and lean back against the door before sliding down to sit. "We've helped so many girls just like you. Some boys too, but they're at another safe house."

"They'll never stop coming."

The mixture of fear and conviction in her voice sends a chill down my spine.

"What do you mean?"

A soft click reaches my ears when she unlocks the door. I scramble to my feet and grip the doorknob.

"Can I come in?" I want her to say it's okay. I've learned that assuming gets me nowhere.

"You can do whatever you want."

I twist the knob and push the door open slowly. Paulina is sitting on the edge of the tub. Her hair is wet, and the borrowed sweats practically hang off her skinny frame. The clothes she was wearing when she arrived at Jacks and Jills are balled up in the corner behind the door.

"I bet that shower felt pretty good," I comment.

She nods.

"Are you hungry?"

Paulina shrugs.

"Have you eaten anything since the club?"

"No."

"Why don't you come out to the kitchen, and we'll get you something to eat?"

She shakes her head so hard I'm afraid she's going to give herself whiplash. "I can't."

Alarm bells go off in my head. "How come?" When she doesn't say anything, I take a step toward her. "What is it, Paulina?"

"They know who I am."

"Who does?"

"Them," she says and nods in the direction of the living room.

"The other girls?"

Paulina nods.

"No." I shake my head in an effort to reassure her. "We didn't give them any information. Remember? They were in bed when you arrived, so we didn't do any introductions."

"I know but no introductions were needed," she insists.

"Paulina, I'm not quite following you here."

I take a deep breath to try to keep my frustration at bay.

I'm exhausted and not in the mood to coddle her more than I normally do for any other victim.

"Can you just tell me why you're so scared?"

"They were in the kitchen when I got up. I recognized them immediately, and they recognized me too."

"So you all know each other?"

"Yes," she snaps. "I…"

Paulina drops her chin and stares at the floor.

"You what?"

When she lifts her head and locks eyes with me, I see tears shimmering in their depths.

"I helped lure them in."

Well, fuck.

"Do you really think leaving her there was the best decision?"

I pop a gummy bear into my mouth and chew it, wishing the THC it's infused with would hit faster than it does. Edibles are great for those times we're in public and I can't simply light up, but damn if they don't take forever to kick in.

I stare past Mollie and watch as cars drive by the outdoor patio of the deli we're at. It's getting close to rush hour, and the traffic is picking up, as well as the insistent honking of horns. This is why I hate the city. Not only do the cage-drivers hog the road among themselves, add a Harley to the traffic and they think they own the streets.

"If there was another option…" I begin. "No, it wouldn't be the best decision. But what other options are there?"

Mollie sucks on the straw in her strawberry shake. After swallowing, she says, "I don't think you really want an answer to that question."

"Does your answer have anything to do with a cer—"

"You know it does," she snaps, frustration taking over, and slams her glass on the table. "Fuck, LT. This isn't about you and your stupid grudge."

"Watch it, Mol," I snarl as I rise from my chair and lean forward. "I've made my position clear, and I expect you, and the others, to respect it."

"You're right, you have made it clear… fucking crystal." She stands. "But I wouldn't be a very good VP, or best friend for that matter, if I didn't challenge you when you're making a huge goddamn mistake."

"Ladies." A waiter steps up next to our table and frowns. "This is a family establishment. Please keep that in mind."

"Fuck off," I bark and turn in a circle to look at the other deli customers sitting at the tables around us. All of them avert their eyes. "If any of you have a problem with the way we talk, you can go fuck yourselves."

I pull some cash from my pocket and flick a twenty at the waiter. It flitters toward the ground, but he snatches it up before it can blow away.

"Let's get outta here, Mol."

I storm away, my boots thudding on the pavement in perfect rhythm with the steady drum of my heartbeat in my ears. Mollie falls into step beside me within seconds. We walk in silence to the public lot where we left our Harleys.

"Would you stop?!" Mollie shouts before we reach the bikes.

I stop in my tracks and turn to face her. "What?"

Mollie's shoulders slump, and her face softens. "It's been six years, L—"

"I'm aware," I bark.

"Let me finish." She steps up to her Harley and throws a leg over the seat. "It's been six years. Six fucking years, Luna. Don't you think it's time you forgive him, forgive yourself? Isn't it time to put the pain aside and do what's best for these girls and the club?" She takes a deep breath but continues before I can say anything. "Don't you think it's time to stop letting emotion control your decisions and get justice for Delia?"

When I remain silent, Mollie cranks the engine of her bike. She stares at me a moment longer before she pulls away, leaving me standing here feeling like she shoved a knife into my heart and twisted it. I let my head fall back and look up at the sky. A shiver races through me at the words that are carried on the wind, in the distinct voice of my mother.

It's time, my love.

CHAPTER SEVEN

Death is coming.

Riker

Six years and one month earlier...

"Yes, sir."

I force a smile as I stare down at the sub kneeling at my feet. She's a pretty little thing. Petite, blonde… and fucking stacked. And she's not even close to my type. Other than being submissive, that is.

She's also not the woman I booked the playroom for. But Delia texted me an hour ago and said the other sub cancelled and asked if I was okay with a replacement. I wanted to tell her no, but my balls had other ideas. So here I am, standing above a sub who is doing her best to please me, but failing miserably.

"I'm so exci—"

"Silence," I snap, and she presses her lips together before lowering her gaze to the floor. "Did I give you permission to speak?"

She shakes her head.

"I can't fucking hear you."

When she starts to shake her head again, I crouch down and grip her chin between my fingers and force her head up.

"What part of 'I can't fucking hear you' made you think shaking your head again is okay?"

Tears brim in her eyes, and disgust rolls through me. Not at her. At myself. Delia warned me that this sub was inexperienced. I knew when I closed that door that she would be my responsibility. Yet here I am, getting inexplicably pissed because she's so damn green.

I let go of her and stand, taking a deep breath as I do. After a moment, I feel slightly calmer. Okay, that's a lie. I'm not even close to calm, but I do feel like I won't take it out on this poor woman.

"Stand up," I command her.

It takes a moment, but she complies. She clasps her hands behind her back and keeps her head lowered.

"I'm hitting the pause button," I tell her, and her shoulders immediately relax, which tells me I'm making the right call.

"I'm really sorry, sir," she says quietly.

A chuckle bursts from me, but there's no humor in it. "You can drop the sir. We're paused, so it's okay."

"Yes, s—" She closes her mouth and then lets out a small laugh. "I, um, I don't know what to call you."

"Jesus, she didn't even give you my real name?"

That's not like Delia. She always remembers details, big or small, and makes a point to ensure members and newbies get the info they need. That's why Jacks and Jills is so successful. Because Delia doesn't fuck up… not ever.

"No, she didn't."

She flicks her gaze toward the door and then returns her eyes to mine. Her lips part, but no words come out.

"You can say whatever you have to say. When we're paused, you can speak freely."

She nods. "Right. Sorry, sir." I grit my teeth to stop myself from correcting her. "Um, when I got here, Delia seemed preoccupied with someone."

I narrow my eyes. "Who?"

"I'm not sure." She shrugs. "They seemed to know each other, though. They sat at the bar and talked while I filled out my paperwork. And once I was done, she pointed me toward this room and that was it."

While it doesn't make sense as far as what I normally expect from Delia, it doesn't necessarily mean anything. It's Sunday, which is typically reserved for Platinum Doms and Delia to utilize the playrooms without the normal crowd of members. I signed up for an earlier slot than I usually do because I've got Soulless Kings business to handle in a few hours, and I need some relief beforehand. All I was made privy to with regards to Delia's schedule is that she booked a room with another dom, one who she was comfortable switching with.

I shake the thoughts from my head. They're irrelevant. What Delia does and who she does it with isn't my business.

"My name is Dominic," I tell her, finally circling back to the original conversation.

She snorts. "Seriously?" she asks, and her lips tilt into a grin.

I narrow my eyes at her. "Yeah, seriously. What the fuck is so funny about that?"

"Nothing, it's just…" She shakes her head, and her grin disappears. "You're a dom and your name is Dominic."

"You can call me Riker," I snap. I immediately want to call back the words, or at least the annoyance with which they were said. Once again, I'm irrationally upset about something that isn't her fault. "What's your name? I didn't get that from Delia."

"Heidi."

"Are you ready to unpause, Heidi?" I ask, needing to get back to the roles we're meant to play.

Heidi spreads her feet shoulder width apart, lowers her head, and clasps her hands behind her back.

"Yes, sir."

"Good girl." I lift her chin with my finger and smile, fully embracing the person I'm supposed to be to her. "What's your safe word?"

"I don't have one, sir," she answers honestly, causing me to frown.

"What's something you're afraid of?"

"Death." That one word comes quickly.

"Okay." I nod my understanding. "If you reach your limit, at any time or for any reason, all you have to do is say 'Death is coming' and I'll stop. Do you understand."

"Yes, sir."

"Good girl." I drop my hand and square my shoulders. "Kneel," I command.

Heidi drops to her knees in perfect sub fashion. I drop my gaze to take her in, praying for my cock to join my brain and get into the scene.

"Take your top off."

Heidi quickly pulls her shirt over her head, exposing a rack encased in lace that would knock most men off their feet. Unfortunately, it does nothing for me… yet.

"I need to see those tits," I snarl. "Now!"

Heidi takes her bra off and tosses it to the floor next to her. Her nipples pebble under my scrutiny, and still, my dick doesn't join the party. I unsnap my jeans and shove them and my boxer briefs down my legs. I'd rid myself of my boots and socks when I got here to avoid getting slowed down by them at an inopportune time. I kick my legs free.

"Look at me," I demand.

Heidi lifts her head, but her gaze stops at my cock, and she licks her lips. I don't know what the fuck she's so turned on for. My dick isn't cooperating, so it's less than impressive at the moment.

"Sir, I can help with that, if you'd like."

Yes, I'd fucking like!

"Give it all you've got."

She does. Heidi sucks me off like she was born to give head. And yet, even after coming in her mouth and making sure her needs are taken care of, when she leaves the room, all I feel is relief.

Relief that the scene is over. Relief that she's gone. Relief that I achieved release, even if I was picturing another dirty little sub while it was happening. Relief that I can now focus on Soulless Kings shit because half of my soul has been fed.

I briefly consider taking advantage of the shower in the attached bathroom but decide against it. I need to get out of here and back to my real life.

I turn off the 'in use' light before exiting the room and close the door behind me. I walk into the main area of the club and see it empty.

"Delia!" I call out.

When there's no response, I walk down the other hallway, in the direction of the room she typically uses. The 'in use' light is lit outside her door. I could try to get her attention, but the rooms are soundproof so it wouldn't do any good. I shoot her a quick text to let her know I left and head out.

CHAPTER EIGHT

Something isn't right.

Luna

Same day...

"Luna, my love, this is not how we do things."

I roll my eyes at the censure in my mother's tone. She almost always tacks on 'my love', and I like it. Unless of course, she's using her you're-letting-me-down tone, as she is now.

"Mom, I'm an adult," I whine.

I'm fully aware that I don't sound like one. But dammit, she's always trying to match me with doms she thinks I'll like. And since it's never the one I actually want, I found *myself* a dom to play with. I glance over my shoulder at the man sitting in the F-250 behind me.

When he hit on me at the bar, I was annoyed. Who the fuck hits on someone at a bar on a Sunday afternoon? He does apparently, and it seems I'm pretty okay with that. It didn't take long for him to see something in me indicating I'm a submissive. Any dom worth their salt can usually tell.

And when I noticed him noticing, I laid it on thick. Anything to get out of another match made by my mother. We exchanged names, pleasantries, and soon we'll be exchanging body fluid.

I cringe internally at my own thoughts. If my mother could hear me now?

I signal to Brandon that I'll only be another minute and he crooks his finger letting me know I need to hurry it up. My pussy clenches at the motion. Gah, I can't wait to feel that finger crooking inside of me.

"I am fully aware you're an adult," she snaps, pulling me back to my phone call. "But it took a lot for me to—"

My mother's words are cut off by what sounds like someone in the background. She must have put her hand over the phone because all the sound is muffled, and I can't make out what they're saying to each other. You've got to be kidding me. I don't have time for this shit.

"Mom?" No response. "Mom?!" I shout into the cell.

"Sorry, my love," she says a moment later. "I gotta go. If you insist on not following through with the dom I secured for you, at least wear a rubber with the dick you picked up at the bar."

I chuckle at her. She may seem okay with my decision, but she's gotta throw out one last dig.

"I will," I assure her. "Love you."

I disconnect the call before she can respond and shove the phone in my back pocket. I turn and walk toward the truck, grinning at Brandon through the windshield.

"You good to go babe?" he asks when I open the passenger door.

I climb into the cab and pull the door shut. "Sure am." I

put my seatbelt on and turn to face him. "You sure you don't mind bringing me back to my bike?"

Brandon spares a glance at my Harley in his rearview mirror. "Not at all."

"Then take me to your dungeon, master."

I mean the words as a joke, something to lighten the mood, but all he does is give me a funny look and turn the key in the ignition. Brandon pulls away from the curb and heads in the direction of what I later learned is in fact a dungeon… in the basement of the house where he lives with, get this, his fucking mother.

Four hours later, Brandon parks next to the curb to drop me off. He's sporting a grin that hasn't left his face since the second he walked me down the rickety wooden steps to his 'playroom'. The only difference in it now is that there's a giant helping of satisfaction in the grin.

Turns out, Brandon likes to dominate, but he's not exactly attentive to his submissives. In fact, he doesn't give a shit about them. My lust died hours ago, and the moment it did, I wished I would have kept the meeting at Jacks and Jills.

But I didn't. And now I need to find another way to get release before my body detonates. After Brandon peels out of the parking space and down the road, I climb on my Harley and fire it up. The rumble between my thighs ratchets up the need for release. I wiggle on the seat a few times before accepting the fact that it's going to be a long and uncomfortable ride to Jacks and Jills.

When I pull into the employee lot at the back of the club, the only thing I can think about is getting inside and seeing if there are still doms here who would be willing to give me a little of their time. I race across the pavement, sparing a glance at my mom's Harley parked in its usual spot close to the building.

I yank open the door and am plunged into the loud beat of some song I don't recognize.

What the fuck?

There is never music playing on Sundays because we aren't open to all members. The only music that should be playing is any a dom or sub want to listen to in their private rooms and even then, I wouldn't hear it because of the soundproofing.

I look down the hallway and see that the light in the main room is off. Security lights are the only thing making it possible for me to see.

My senses tingle and goosebumps break out over my skin.

Something isn't right.
Something isn't right.
Something isn't right.

Those three words play on a loop in my head as I bend to grab one of the knives out of my boot. For a brief second an image of the panicked look on Brandon's face when he saw my weapons enters my mind, but I quickly shove it away. There will be time to laugh at his expense later when I recount my day to Mollie.

With my fingers wrapped around the handle, I lift the blade up next to my head, preparing to strike if necessary.

Something isn't right.
Something isn't right.
Something isn't right.

I turn the corner at the end of the hall and step into the main room. In the minimal lighting, I see no one. I run to the ends of the other hallways and search for an 'in' use' light but I come up empty.

What. The. Fuck?

"Mom!" I shout, loud enough to be heard over the music.

No answer.

I walk to the middle of the main room and turn in circles.

"C'mon, Mom, this isn't funny."

Still, no answer.

Just as I'm about to lower my knife and pull out my cell phone, a shadow catches my attention by the bar, and I squint to try and see better.

My heart plummets.

"Mom!"

I run toward her body, and when I see the pool of blood around her head, I drop to my knees, sliding the rest of the way.

"Holy fuck, mom!" I wail.

I shift to my ass and lift her head into my lap. I run my hands over her face, her skull, and find the bullet hole near her ear, hidden slightly by sticky, bloody, hair.

Tears fall from my eyes, unchecked, and I taste the salt from them on my lips. Rocking back and forth, my dead mother's head still in my lap, I sob.

"Mom, mom, mom, mom, mom…"

I have no idea how long I sit there. Maybe minutes, maybe hours. Hell, maybe days. All I know is when I calm myself enough to stand, it takes every ounce of strength I have.

I swipe at my cheeks, clearing the last of my tears and hitting pause on my anguish. There's no time for that now. My mother is dead, and I need to find out who killed her.

I pull my cell phone from my back pocket, and when I look at the screen, I gasp. The device is sticky with blood that must have soaked through my pants when I was sitting. I wipe the screen clean on the front of my jeans, trying not to throw up as I do. I'm not squeamish by any means, but this is different. This is the blood of someone I love, not someone I killed.

After telling Siri to 'call Mollie', I put the speakerphone on and wait for her to answer. While I wait, I go behind the bar to get a bottle of tequila. I'm gonna need it.

I take a swig of the liquor, savoring the burn of it sliding down my throat. Mollie's voicemail picks up, and I redial immediately. This is not the time for her to be unreachable.

"C'mon, Mol," I mumble to the ringing cell and drop my head to stare at the floor. "Answer your fucking ph—"

What the hell is that?

I crouch down to see if I can make out the smears in the blood, and sure as rain is wet, I can. Right there, in crimson streaks I can only assume my mother made as she was taking her last breaths are a few letters: C, O, N, R, T.

"Hello!" Mollie's voice pulls me from my trance. "Luna, is everything okay?"

I shake my head even as I'm still trying to make sense of the letters. At the same time I realize she can't see me, everything clicks into place.

"Conrad Templeton."

CHAPTER NINE

Luna McAllister is the female version of me.

Riker
Present day...

"You need to take a break."

I scrub my hands over my face and roll my neck. Squirrel is probably right. We've been at this for days, and I'm beyond exhausted. Not to mention, tense as hell. I stretch my arms above my head, and a putrid odor hits my nostrils.

You fucking stink too.

"Meet back here in two hours?" I ask, looking from Squirrel to Trainwreck and back again.

Two hours isn't a lot of time, but I can grab a shower, a sandwich and hopefully a few minutes of shut eye. Oh, and make a certain apology call I've been putting off.

"Works for me," Trainwreck says. "I'm gonna go take a ride, clear my head." He walks toward the door. "See ya fucks in a bit."

After he leaves the room, Squirrel focuses his attention on me. His stare makes me feel like I'm being examined, and I don't like it. It makes me twitchy.

"What?" I snap.

"Nothing." He shakes his head and works on shutting down his laptop.

"That stare isn't *nothing*," I argue. "If you have something to say, fucking say it."

"It's just… I don't know. You seem different."

Yeah, I've got a set of blue balls that won't quit. And some crazy fucker is out there abducting and selling people.

"I'm not."

I can hear the lie in my voice, and if I can, so can Squirrel.

"Bullshit." He stands and shoves his laptop in his bag. "Look, bro, I get why Trainwreck is obsessed with Templeton. He's responsible for his sister's kidnapping and ruining their family. But you? It doesn't make sense."

Annoyance hits me in the gut like a sucker punch. "Why doesn't it make sense? Templeton is evil. He claims to be some sort of messiah and uses people's belief in religion and their faith to get them to commit some of the worst sins a human can commit. He convinces them they're doing the right thing. Why the hell wouldn't that piss me off or deserve the club's wrath and attention?"

"Not buying it," he quips.

"You don't have to."

I storm past him, ignoring his protests. If he can't understand why I'd take this personally, fuck him. Just because it wasn't my sister who was taken and sold doesn't mean I shouldn't be disgusted or affected by it.

As I walk through the main house, I acknowledge a few brothers with a nod. When they try to call me over to the bar, I shake my head and make my way outside. I step onto the porch and inhale deeply, letting the fresh air wash over me.

I jog down the steps, toward my Harley, but before I reach it, my phone vibrates in my pocket. Stopping in my tracks, I take my cell out and glance at the screen. The notification shows a text from an unknown number.

Unknown: Is this the right number for Dominic Young?

I rack my brain as I stare at the phone number, but for the life of me, I can't figure out who it is.

Me: Who the fuck is this?

Unknown: Is this Dominic?

Me: Depends...

Unknown: I'll take that as a yes. Meet me at Jacks and Jills, tomorrow 8am

Me: Not gonna happen

Unknown: If I told you this is about Delia's murder, would that change your mind?

My grip on the device tightens. Of course it makes a difference, but they don't need to know that. I shove my phone back into my pocket and mount my bike. If whoever the fuck this is wants to play games, I'll play. My first move… making them wait and wonder if I'm going to respond.

I head in the direction of my one-bedroom cabin that sits on the back edge of the property. It doesn't take long to get there, and once I'm inside, I strip out of my clothes and head for the shower.

Stepping under the spray, I tip my head back and let the water sluice over my face, down my body. Memories of Delia assail me, snagging their claws into my thoughts and holding them hostage. As I scrub myself clean, I remember the moment I found out she was dead.

"What happened to Delia?" I ask.

The chick shoves my arm away, and any emotion I think I saw disappears as her face hardens. "She's dead."

A bullet to the chest wouldn't have taken me more by surprise. I haven't heard from Delia in a while, but... dead? When? How?

And why the fuck didn't I know about this before now?

"Nice try," I taunt, not wanting to believe what she's telling me. "You've got two seconds to open that fucking door and take me to Delia." I point to the second entry door behind her.

"What part of dead don't you understand?" she snaps back.

Bitch's two seconds are up. I reach behind my back to grab the pistol I always carry, but before I can wrap my fingers around the butt of the gun, a blade is pressed to my throat.

"I suggest you rethink that," the redhead snarls, her perfect white teeth barred.

I arch a brow, and she increases the pressure on my neck, forcing me back a step to avoid having a permanent scar as a result of her brand of crazy. When my back hits the wall, I lower my arm so she can see I'm no longer reaching for a weapon.

We stare at each other for several tense moments, my heart racing and her chest heaving.

"You can put that down," I tell her.

She tilts her head. "I could, but I don't want to."

"Fair enough."

I scramble to come up with a way to get her to lower the knife, anything to reverse the power dynamic. An idea hits me, one so obvious that a fresh wave of anger courses through me for not having thought of it before.

"I've seen you around Jacks and Jills," I say, letting the dom in me take over. I give her a sly grin. "But I don't think we've officially met."

"And...?"

"You're a sub, right?"

Immediately, her eyes lower, but she quickly hardens her expression again so all I see is hate. It's a look I'm used to... that one a submissive gets when their body begs for one thing, but their mind isn't quite on board.

"Answer me," I demand, letting lust ooze into my tone.

She shakes her head.

"I can't hear you."

"No, I'm not a fucking sub!" she shouts.

Unfortunately for her, she can't look me in the eye when she yells, which tells me just how hard she's fighting her instincts.

"I beg to differ, baby girl."

Her head whips up, and her eyes lock on mine.

"You need to leave."

"And that's not your call to make."

The redhead tilts her head and smirks. "If I told you I was Delia's daughter, would that change your mind?"

Pain radiates through my hand when I crash my fist into the fiberglass shower surround.

Holy. Fucking. Shit!

I rush to finish my shower and when I turn the water off and step over the edge of the tub, I wrap a towel around my waist. Not bothering to dry any of the excess water sliding over my skin, I race into my bedroom and pick up my earlier discarded jeans.

I grab my cell from the pocket and tap on the screen to bring it to life. Quickly opening the texting app, I pull up the text exchange between myself and the unknown number. I reread the texts, which only makes my suspicion stronger and then type a quick message.

Me: Is this Delia's daughter, Luna?

In a matter of seconds, three little dots pop up on the screen and then her response appears: yes.

I was already going to head to Jacks and Jills in the morning, but this new realization spurs my sense of urgency.

Me: Why wait until tomorrow? Meet me in an hr?

Luna: I'll be there.

Little do I know that I'm about to meet a woman so enamored with death and destruction that I begin to worry about my own sanity and safety… because Luna McAllister is the female version of me.

CHAPTER TEN

I don't know how things roll with the Soulless Kings, but here, I'm in charge.

Luna

"What made you change your mind?"

I turn my head from the security monitors in my office to look at Mollie. Ever since I told her I reached out to Riker, she's planted her ass in one of the chairs at my desk. She's asked the same question at least a dozen times and my answer is always the same.

I shrug and return my attention back to the monitors.

"Bullshit," she counters and stands. "For six years, you've wanted nothing to do with him. Hell, you've blamed him. And now, all of a sudden, you're waiting for him to arrive like this is some big summit meeting and you two hold the key to saving the world."

A headlight catches my attention on the monitor that shows me the parking lot, and when I squint to see what caused it, my stomach flips over on itself. He's here.

He pulls into the lot on his Harley like he owns the place.

After parking in a spot close to the road, he stands and starts to take off his cut. As if thinking better of it, he leaves it on and struts across the pavement. His head swivels constantly, no doubt taking in his surroundings because he doesn't trust that he's alone. He knocks on the door when he reaches it, and, as instructed, Spooks lets him in.

I shift my gaze to another monitor and see him in the entryway between the two doors. A grin spreads on my face when I see Spooks give him a hard time about not having a membership ID. She glances toward the camera and winks, and I can't stop the chuckle that escapes. When his shoulders stiffen, my chuckle turns into a full-blown laugh.

"You're enjoying this way too much," Mollie comments.

"And you're trying to kill my vibe," I snap. "You can go."

"Seriously?" she asks in a huff.

"Go take over for Spooks so she can bring him up," I order her without taking my eyes off the monitor. I press the intercom button that allows me to communicate with the front desk. "Let him in, Spooks."

Riker turns in a circle and looks at the corners of the ceiling, no doubt looking for the cameras. He won't find them. I made sure of that.

"I'm not leaving," Mollie grits out. "This isn't just about you, ya know? All of us were affected by Del—"

"Get out!" I shout.

Mollie's face falls, and hurt enters her eyes, flashing emotion-filled fire. I instantly regret being so harsh with her, but I can't let myself worry about that, about her… not right now anyway. She turns and flees, her boots thudding madly on the steps, and I make a mental note to fix things with her later.

Another set of footsteps on the stairs reaches my ears, and my shoulders stiffen. These ones are heavier, less rushed. These belong to *him*.

Spooks steps through the doorway first, Riker right behind her. I itch to smooth out my clothes, make sure I look okay, but I ignore the impulse. This meeting isn't about winning him over or impressing him. I just wish my traitorous pussy knew that.

"Thanks, Spooks," I say with a smile. "I'll take it from here."

Spooks looks from me to Riker and back again. "You sure? I don't mind sticking around for a few."

"She's sure," Riker barks without taking his eyes off of me.

I chew on the inside of my cheek until the metallic taste of blood hits my tongue, and then I chastise myself for it. This is my club, my rules. Spooks is my girl, not his.

"Don't you ever do that again," I snarl as I walk around my desk. "You aren't in charge here. I am."

Riker says nothing, and I turn to Spooks.

"I'm sure," I tell her. "Go back to your post. I'll let you know if I need you."

Spooks doesn't move for several long seconds, but finally, she leaves my office and descends the stairs. When I hear the door at the bottom click shut, I gesture toward a chair.

"Have a seat," I urge him.

"You said this was about Delia's murder," he says flatly and crosses his arms over his chest.

"Sit. Down."

Riker arches a brow but remains on his feet.

"Are you always this stubborn or do you reserve it for me?"

His eyes drop from mine to my chest and then lower still. My insides quiver under his stare, and I have to remind myself that this is not what I had in mind when I reached out to him. Sure, there was a time I would have begged for his domination, but that was a long time ago.

"Well?" I ask.

"Nothing I do is for you, baby girl," he says as he locks eyes with me. "I just don't take orders from a chick."

Anger fans the flames rolling through my veins. "I don't know how things roll with the Soulless Kings, but here, I'm in charge." I lean forward on my desk. "Now, either sit the fuck down or get the fuck out."

Both of his brows shoot up to his hairline. I can't tell if it's shock or respect in his eyes, but either is fine with me. Riker drops his arms and flops down in the chair.

"Don't mistake this for submission," he tells me. "That's not my thing."

As if I could ever mistake him for being submissive.

"Noted." I straighten.

"So…" He rests a booted foot on his knee. "What could you possibly need from me? If I'm not mistaken, you've refused to let me even step foot inside this club since your mom died."

"She didn't die," I snap. "She was murdered."

He waves his hand as if the distinction doesn't matter. Well, I've got news for him… it fucking matters.

"Fine. What do you need from me?"

I glance at the security monitors, the action centering me. When I return my attention to Riker, I see his narrowed eyes have followed mine.

"You sit up here and watch everything?" he asks, judgement dripping from the words.

"If by sit up here and watch everything you mean do I sit up here and make sure that my business is being run and handled appropriately, then yes, I do."

He whips his gaze back to mine. "That's not what I meant."

"Look, I don't need to explain myself to you. How I run this club isn't something you need to trouble yourself with."

"Six years ago, I'd have agreed with that. But then you

banned all MC's from being members. How you run this club directly affects me, so yeah, I'm gonna trouble myself with it." He looks back at the monitors, pointing toward the one that's focused on one of the hallways. "And letting the likes of him in tells me you have no fucking clue what you're doing."

I look at the screen before lifting my iPad off my desk and pulling up the virtual waiting room. I tap on the device until I find what I'm looking for.

"What's wrong with Javier Bloom?" I ask, hating that I have to but needing to know what the hell he's talking about.

He narrows his eyes at me. "You don't know?"

"Would I have asked you if I did?"

"Javier Bloom is one small piece to a very large, complicated puzzle."

"What the hell is that supposed to mean?"

Riker stands. "Baby girl, if you have to ask, then we have nothing to talk about."

CHAPTER ELEVEN

Guilt. It's a funny word, an odd feeling. I don't experience it often… I can't afford to.

Riker

"Wait!"

I stop just before reaching the door, but I don't look over my shoulder at the redhead. Luna said she wanted to talk about her mother's murder, but she obviously has no clue what that actually means.

"Give me one good reason why I should stick around," I demand, still not turning around.

"Because you owe it to my mother… considering she's dead because of you."

Murderous rage swirls in my system, the pressure building to the point where nothing I do will stop it from escaping. I whirl around and stalk toward her, my eyes wide, my muscles tense, my entire body ready to kill.

Somehow, my synapses fire enough to stop me in my tracks before I reach her and wrap my fingers around the column of her throat. I shake my head to clear the red haze from my vision and stare at her.

"Why the fuck are you just standing there?" I bark, annoyed that she isn't doing anything to stop me from attacking her.

"I'm not."

Luna lifts her hand and waves the gun she's holding in my face. I narrow my eyes, glaring at the steel weapon, the one I didn't even notice she grabbed because I was so singularly focused on my rage.

"So," she begins. "My mother's death is a trigger for you." She tilts her head. "Why is that? Guilt, maybe?"

Guilt. It's a funny word, an odd feeling. I don't experience it often… I can't afford to. My lifestyle, my club, demands some pretty fucked up shit of me. Shit I don't give a second thought to. Murder, drugs, guns, violence, mayhem. It's all a part of my everyday life.

"Guilt is a luxury I can't afford," I tell her.

Luna takes a step forward and presses the gun to my stomach. I let her. Like I said, guilt is funny.

"If you *ever* come at me again," Luna snarls. "I won't hesitate to pull the trigger. Got it?"

My cock responds before I can spit words out. Apparently, a fucked-in-the-head chick does it for me as much as a submissive one does. I reach down to adjust myself, and my hand brushes over hers. I feel her tremble at the contact, and when she lowers the gun, I arch a brow.

"What's wrong, baby girl?" I taunt.

Rather than answer me, she turns to walk back to her desk and sets the pistol down. Her hands are shaking when she runs them through her hair, tousling the red locks. I flex my hands and try to ignore the impulse to close the distance between us and muss up her hair myself.

The silence that ensues is deafening and only broken by the crackling of the speaker system.

"Looney Tunes, code black."

"Fuck!" Luna shouts and bangs a fist on her desk. She starts toward the door leading to the staircase and stabs a finger in the air at me. "Stay here."

Not happening.

I rush to follow her, catching up to her at the bottom of the steps. She glares at me, but before Luna can chastise me for not listening, we're joined by two other women, both wearing the same cut.

"You know better than to use the speakers for this shit," Luna bites out at them.

"I texted you," one of them says with bitterness in her tone. She cuts her eyes to me and then back to Luna. "You didn't answer."

Luna pulls her cell out of her pocket and taps the screen. She mutters under her breath before pocketing it again. She turns to the chick who said she texted her.

"Mollie, get Spooks to lock the place down. No one gets in or out unless I give the okay."

"Someone care to fill me in?" I ask.

Luna spins on her heel and glares at me. "I told you to stay put," she seethes.

"And I didn't listen." I shrug. "Do you really want to argue about this?"

Luna turns to look toward the front entrance, and I follow her gaze. There's another chick with the same cut standing there with her arm around a kid.

A kid? Why the hell is a kid here?

When Luna's eyes return to mine, I can see the indecision in them, the questions plaguing her expression. Should she trust me? Can I keep a secret? Do I know what's going on?

These aren't questions she needs to voice because they're the same ones I ask myself when I'm in a precarious situation.

"You can trust me," I tell her, lowering my voice so only she can hear it over the music. "Now, what can I do to help?"

It's not lost on me that, for some reason, Luna links me to her mother's murder, to the unknown of it all, and yet, here I am, asking her to set that aside so I can help her with whatever the fuck is going on. It's not lost on me that I *want* to help her, that I *need* to help her.

Luna's eyes shift from mine to the other chick still standing next to her. "Libs, head to the southern safe house and prep a room." She takes a deep breath and quickly glances at me. "Riker and I got it from here."

Libs hesitates for a moment. I get it. She doesn't know me, and this is something that is no doubt club business, nothing outsiders are normally privy to. But she was given an order by her President, and she'll follow it.

"I swear on my mother's grave, if you don't follow my lead and do exactly as I say, I will end you." Luna's hands are wrapped in my shirt, almost as if she's trying to lift me up. "Got it?"

"Got it."

She drops her arms. "Good. Let's go."

I follow Luna to the entrance, making sure to always be aware of our surroundings. It wouldn't do anyone any good if Jacks and Jills' members tried to step in or question what's going on. When we reach the front, Luna's entire demeanor changes.

"Hi," she says to the kid. "I'm Luna."

The kid lifts their head and looks at me. Okay, not just a kid… a boy, no older than nine or ten. The little boy sniffles and wipes his nose with the sleeve of his shirt.

"His name is Riker," Luna tells him. "You can trust him."

Huh?

"Ah, Looney Tunes," the woman says. "Can I talk to you for a sec?"

Luna gives a curt nod and stands. "Hey, dude. Can you do me a huge favor?"

He shrugs.

"I need you to stay here with Riker, make sure he behaves. Can you do that for me?"

"Sure," he mumbles.

Luna ruffles his hair. "Sweet. Thanks."

I watch Luna and the other chick walk a few feet away, and then they lower their heads to talk. I wish I could hear what they're saying, but the music makes it impossible, so I focus on the kid.

"What's your name?" I ask him.

He doesn't respond. Instead, he stares at me, warily and with fear in his eyes. Kids have never been my forte. Don't get me wrong, I love my brothers' kids, all of them, but I'm not the best at relating to them.

"Okay, you don't feel like talking." I cross my arms loosely over my chest. "I get that. I'm not a big talker either."

He looks toward Luna and back to me. "I want my mom."

What the hell am I supposed to do about that?

"Do you know where she is?"

He shakes his head.

"Well, I'm sure we can find her." I have no idea if that's true or not, but at this point, I'll say anything.

"He's right, ya know?" Luna says from behind me. I look at her, and she smiles, although I'm fairly certain it's not for me. "We'll find your mom." She steps around me. "While we look for her, how about we get you some clean clothes and something to eat? Are you hungry?"

He nods.

"I imagine you're pretty tired, too, huh?" she says as she reaches for his hand.

When he links his fingers in hers, I see the way his knuckles turn white. Fear will make a person do things they wouldn't normally do, like hang on to a stranger like they're a lifeline.

I follow Luna and the boy to a hallway that leads to the back door of the club. When we step outside, the kid shivers from the chilly night air.

"Here," I say as I take off my cut and then my long-sleeved T-shirt. I hand the garment to him. "This should keep you warm."

He takes it and pulls it over his head. "Thanks."

"No problem, kid."

"Slim," he says.

"What?"

"They call me Slim."

"Ah, okay." I grin. "Is that your real name or a nickname?"

Luna cuts a scathing look in my direction. I hold my hands up in a gesture of surrender. Oops. I forgot her rule… follow her lead.

"Slim, we're gonna get you to our safe house and let you eat and get some sleep." Luna urges him toward a waiting van. "We can talk more in the morning."

"Are you coming with me?" he asks, planting his feet just outside the side door of the vehicle.

"Of course," she assures him and then points to the driver. "Mollie here is my best friend, and she's going to take you to our house where we can keep you safe. I'll be right behind you on my bike, okay?"

"What about him?" Slim asks with a quick look at me.

"He's gonna come too, if that's okay with you?" she answers.

I guess I'm not going home tonight.

Slim seems to think about it for a second and then nods. "Okay."

He climbs in the back of the van, and as Luna pulls the door closed, I hear the driver—Mollie—start talking to Slim.

Luna pounds on the side of the van, and it pulls away, out of the back lot. When she turns to me, I drop my kid-friendly expression and demeanor and glare at her.

"What the fuck are you getting me involved in?"

CHAPTER TWELVE

When it comes to my club, my family, these victims? I'm fucking in charge, and Riker better get used to it.

Luna

"Don't you dare walk away from me!"

Riker's tone of voice is like ice water in my veins. He's angry. And if I'm being honest, rightfully so. He came to Jacks and Jills to discuss my mom's murder and now he's being thrust into a problem he didn't ask for.

Unfortunately, I don't have the time to stand around and argue with him or answer his questions. I will, but not here in the parking lot.

"I wouldn't be walking away if you were following me," I call over my shoulder.

A fraction of a second passes before his footsteps thudding across the pavement reaches my ears. He falls into step beside me, but when we reach the door and I grab the handle, he wraps his fingers around my wrist, stopping me.

"You told Slim we were going to the safe house."

I lift my eyes to his, ignoring the way his touch sends flames licking over my flesh. I take a deep breath to steady myself before responding.

"And we will. But I have to lock up my office first." I inject as much snarky attitude into my tone as possible. "Is that okay with you?"

Riker's jaw tenses up, and his cheek twitches. He removes his hand and shoves it through his hair. When his arm flexes with his movement, the tendons ripples under his skin.

He doesn't respond, but instead, grabs the doorknob himself and twists it as he pushes it open. Riker gestures for me to enter ahead of him.

I brush past him and make my way down the hall and into the main room. Surprisingly, there are only a few members left, and even they are making their way out the front entrance. I pull my cell phone out of my pocket and glance at the time. I breathe a sigh of relief when I see that it's close enough to closing time that this won't upset our more prestigious members.

"Why are you closing early?" Riker asks from behind me.

Before I can answer him, Spooks rushes to my side.

"Figured shutting down was the best thing," she says. "Members were getting irritated that they were locked in, and with him here," she nods at Riker and shrugs. "Just made sense to close."

"Good call." I glance at the man standing next to me. I can feel the tension coming off him in waves at her explanation. Too fucking bad. "I'm gonna lock up my office and head to the safe house."

"He going with you?" Spooks asks.

"*He's* standing right here and can answer for himself," Riker snaps.

Spooks grins and lets her gaze drop to take in all of him,

and when her eyes return to his face, she licks her lips. "Yeah, I see you."

Jealousy whips through me, and that only ratchets up my frustration. "Yeah," I say, ignoring the unwelcome feeling. "He's going with me."

Spooks nods and retreats to finish signing out the members and closing up the club. I stride across the main room toward the staircase and then take steps two at a time up to my office. Riker follows close behind.

"Close the door behind you," I order him when we reach the second level.

"For a sub, you're bossy as fuck."

I whirl around, my eyes wide with surprise.

"What?" he asks.

I stare at him a moment longer before shaking my head. "Nothing." I nod toward the door. "Close it."

He does as he's told, chuckling. The sound grates on my nerves, but I try to push past that. I need to get out of here and to the safe house. Slim is the second victim to show up in a few days, and while not unheard of, it is unusual.

I grab my iPad off my desk and check the virtual waiting room. All members have checked out. Next, I look at each of the security monitors and ensure there are no stragglers in the building. Assuring myself that all of the playrooms are empty, I finally relax my shoulders.

"What can I do to help get us out of here faster?" Riker asks.

I double check that the monitors are set to record, as they always should be, and walk back toward him and the door.

"Nothing. We're all set."

We walk out of my office, and I enter the lock code on the wall next to the door before heading back downstairs. When we're on the first floor, I make a beeline for Spooks, who's helping the bartender clean up the bar area.

"We'll be at the south safe house," I tell her. "I need you to make the rounds on the others, make sure everyone is okay."

"You got it."

I turn to the man who is now going to get a glimpse into my world, the world I've done everything in my power to keep hidden.

"Go get your Harley and follow me."

Riker clucks his tongue. "So fucking bossy."

I roll my eyes and walk away from him. I may be a submissive but only under certain circumstances. When it comes to my club, my family, these victims? I'm fucking in charge and Riker better get used to it.

The ride to the safe house feels like it takes hours, but it's only eighteen miles from the club, on the southern outskirts of Portland. When I pull into the driveway, I make my way around to the back of the split-level home and pull into the garage that's built under it. Riker follows behind and parks next to me.

"Nice neighborhood," he comments after we both cut our engines and stand.

"It is."

I turn away from him and go to the door that leads into the mud room off the kitchen. When we step inside, we're immediately greeted by Mollie.

"Where's Slim?" I ask as I lean on the kitchen island.

"He just got out of the shower. He'll be out of the bathroom any minute, I'm sure." Mollie reaches into the cupboard above the dishwasher and pulls down three shot glasses and a bottle of Tequila. She pours the shots and hands them to us. "To a long night," she toasts with her raised glass.

Mollie and I quickly down ours, but Riker stands there with a shell-shocked look on his face.

"Would someone tell me what the hell is going on?" he demands through gritted teeth.

I nod at the glass in his hand. "You gonna drink that?"

When he takes more than a second to answer, I grab it from him and down it myself. I slam the glass on the counter, and that seems to snap him out of it.

"Guess not," he says and crosses his arms over his chest.

A door creaks in the house, and my muscles tense. Footsteps on the hardwood get closer, and then Slim steps through the arched kitchen entrance. His eyes dart from Mollie to me to Riker before they settle on the food-filled plate on the counter.

"Is that for me?" he asks, pointing at it.

"It sure is, bud," Mollie responds and pushes the plate toward him.

Slim hesitates for a moment, but his hunger gets the better of him. When he lets himself go, he devours the food within minutes. He licks the mayo off his fingers that dripped out of the sandwich and gives a sheepish grin when he realizes we're all watching him.

"Sorry," he says and lowers his head.

"For what?" I ask as I walk around the island to sit on the stool next to him.

Slim shrugs. "CT says I eat too fast sometimes."

I glance at Riker out of the corner of my eye and see his shoulders stiffen. I can't tell if the response is to the criticism this little boy has received, to the name CT, or to the entire situation. Regardless, his reaction matches my own, and that makes me realize he might not be a heartless asshole after all.

"You should see me eat a steak," Riker says once he levels out his expression. "Nothing wrong with eating fast, kid. Means you appreciate the food."

Slim leans against the back of the stool he's sitting on and seems to think about that for a minute.

"CT says no one likes a pig, and whether we're eating…" Slim fidgets with his hands as if trying to remember exactly what he's been told. He takes a deep breath and continues. "Whether we're eating our favorite snack or slop, we need to eat slow." Slim shifts his focus to me. "He says our new parents won't like it if we're rude and eat fast."

Mollie and I exchange a look before I respond. "New parents?"

"Uh huh,' Slim confirms. "CT said my first mom and dad gave me to him. He said they wanted to make sure they made it to… to the…" He shakes his head. "I can't remember what he called it."

"Land of Sinfinite Opportunity," Riker says.

Slim nods frantically. "Yeah, that."

Sensing that Riker has way more info than we do, I do what I can to finish my questioning of Slim. I ruffle his hair.

"I bet you're tired," I say to the boy. As if on cue, Slim yawns. A chuckle bubbles up and out of my mouth. "I just have a few more questions and then you can get some sleep. How does that sound?"

Slim nods.

"Okay, good." I take a deep breath and blow it out slowly. "How old are you, Slim?"

"Ten." He narrows his eyes. "No, wait. CT says I'm eleven."

Both ages are way too young in my book. No one should have to go through whatever he went through before showing up at Jacks and Jills, but especially not a kid.

"Do you remember where you lived? Before you lived with CT."

He shakes his head. "But I know my phone number. My mom made me learn it, just in case."

"Good, that's good." I can work with a phone number.

"What about your name, bud? I know people call you Slim, but has that always been your name or did people call you something else before?"

Slim's expression closes up, making me think this is a question he's been taught to fear. Or he's been threatened if he gives his real name.

"Slim, you know you're safe here, right?" I rest my hand on his shoulder and feel a slight tremble in his body. My heart breaks for him. "No one, especially not CT, can get to you."

"You don't know that," he mumbles.

"I do know that, Slim. I've made sure that anyone who comes to us for help can't be found."

"But the bad people are everywhere," he insists.

"The bad people?" I ask for clarification. "You mean CT?"

Slim shakes his head. "Not just him. I saw one of his friends earlier."

Riker, who's remained pretty quiet the last few minutes, leans on the island with a thud of his fists. "Where?" he demands. "Where did you see one of his friends?"

"While I was waiting for the lady to get Looney Tunes."

That's who all of the victims ask for when they arrive. We made sure of that. If they find our strategically placed signs, they're instructed to ask for 'Looney Tunes', for me.

"At the club?" Riker asks. "You saw someone you knew at the club?"

"Uh huh."

"Who?" Riker demands, his tone becoming more impatient, angrier.

Slim hunches his shoulders. Time to put an end to this interrogation and regroup.

"Ya know what, bud," I begin and rub circles over his back. "Why don't you try to get some sleep? We can talk more in the morning."

Riker groans, but I ignore it. I know he wants more information. Shit, so do I. But not at the expense of a little boy who's already scared.

Slim rubs his eyes. "Okay. I *am* tired."

"C'mon, little man," Mollie urges as she steps up behind him and rests her hand on his back. "I'll take you to your room."

Slim hops off the stool and walks out of the kitchen with Mollie. Before they disappear down the hall, he looks over his shoulder.

"Kenny," he says. "My name is Kenny."

CHAPTER THIRTEEN

How the fuck am I supposed to show her she can trust me?

Riker

Sitting on the stool Slim vacated, I wait patiently for Luna to give me some fucking answers. What started out as a meeting to talk about Delia has turned into… I don't even know what.

"You're surprisingly quiet."

I narrow my eyes at Luna, who is now throwing back her third shot of Tequila since Mollie took Slim out of the kitchen. When she sets the glass down, I wait for her to ask if I want one, but she doesn't.

This isn't a social call.

"Why did you get so upset when Slim mentioned CT?" she asks me, tilting her head.

"Should we really be calling him Slim?" I counter. "Especially if it's a name his abductor gave him?"

"What do you know about abductors?"

"More than I fucking care too," I mumble.

I reach across the island and snag the Tequila and her empty shot glass. I pour myself a shot and down it in one burning gulp. Without slowing down, I pour another and shoot it back. Afterward, I lock eyes with Luna and wait her out.

She's the first to break eye contact and when she lowers her gaze to the counter, my cock twitches behind my fly. I shift on the stool in an effort to get more comfortable but it's impossible. It seems, where this chick is concerned, comfort is too much to hope for.

When Luna lifts her head, there's a sheen to her eyes. Her face is hard, like she's trying to fight whatever emotion is coming over her, but she's failing miserably.

"What's wrong?" I ask, the question coming out harsher than I'd like.

Luna inhales deeply and laughs without humor. "You'd think I'd be used to this."

"To what?"

She waves her hand. "This," she snaps. "The victims, the kids, the stories. After six years, I should be able to handle it."

"What exactly is it that you've been doing for six years?"

It seems obvious but I've learned to never make assumptions.

Lula pulls her bottom lip between her teeth for a second before answering. "When my mom died, we figured out pretty quickly who was behind the murder. After some digging, things began to link up to human traffickers." Her face falls and she shrugs. "I couldn't save my mom so I decided that Devil's Handmaidens—our chapter anyway— would focus on saving as many victims of human trafficking as we can."

The urge to reach out and comfort her is strong but I shove it down. I'm not here to comfort her. Come to think of it, I'm not exactly sure why I'm here.

"Speaking of Delia," I begin. "You said you wanted to talk to me about the night she died."

Almost instantly, Luna's demeanor shifts from vulnerable woman to pissed off bitch. The change is fascinating, and I can't help but wonder about the ways she'd change from domineering MC president and club owner to submissive partner in the bedroom… or any other room for that matter.

Luna walks around the island and into the living room, leaving me to follow. I get the sense that she expects me to and that rubs me the wrong way, but not for the first time tonight, I push the frustration aside.

I sit next to her on the couch, and she immediately gets up and begins pacing.

"Look, I've got better things to do than wa—"

"What do you know about Conrad Templeton?" she blurts out.

A big part of me knew the name would come up but there's something about it coming out of her mouth that disturbs me. And as much as I want to deny any and all knowledge of the man, I realize that there is no part of me that wants to lie to her.

"I know he's bad news," I tell her, unsure how much information to divulge. I don't want to lie but I certainly don't want to give away everything the Soulless Kings know.

"Did you see him that night?" she shouts, coming to a stop next to the couch. "Did you let him into Jacks and Jills?" Her arms are flailing as she slings accusations. "Did you enjoy her screams for help?"

I shoot to my feet and stalk toward her. Her eyes widen and she retreats a few steps, but I manage to grab hold of her arms when she backs into the wall.

"What the fuck are you talking about?"

With my hands around her wrists, Luna tries to pound on my chest. She thrashes and kicks and yells.

"Would you two keep it down?!" Mollie whispers harshly as she races into the room. She takes in the scene before her and rolls her eyes. "If you can't be quiet, take it outside."

"I'm not some child you—"

Luna yanks out of my hold, pulling my attention from Mollie. Her breathing is labored but at least she's settling down.

"She's right," Luna says breathily and glares at me. "I don't like being told what to do but, in this case, Mollie's right." Luna starts to walk to the door that I know leads to the garage. "Riker, you can either come talk to me outside or get the fuck off the property. Up to you."

My feet don't budge, almost as if they're anchored to the floor with concrete. Mollie's sigh breaks the tension in the room, and I turn away from where Luna disappeared around the corner and look at her.

"I will deny having said this until I take my last breath but don't let her fool you." Mollie brushes a strand of hair out of her face. "She's not as hardened and bitchy as she seems."

"You sure about that?"

Mollie chuckles. "Not always." She takes a few steps toward me. "The thing about Luna…"

"What about her?" I ask when her eyes dart toward the door as if she expects Luna to pop back in any second.

"Nothing," she says quickly and turns away from me. "I need to check on everyone."

With that, she disappears down the hall, leaving me there to figure out what the fuck she was trying to tell me. Clearly, she doesn't want me to think Luna's a bitch. And if I'm being honest with myself, I don't. I'm not sure I'm ready to admit that to Luna but there you have it.

I slowly make my way out of the house. I stop at my Harley and debate just firing it up and getting the fuck out of here. I can take what I've learned to the Soulless Kings and forget about Luna and Delia and what they have to do with any of it. Dismissing the idea, I exit the garage and search for Luna.

I spot a gravel path at the edge of the yard and decide to follow it. With Luna nowhere in sight in the yard immediately around the home, this is the only logical way she could have gone. After passing some trees, the surroundings seem to open up, revealing a large pond with a dock.

At the end of the dock, with her knees pulled up to her chest, is Luna. She's leaning against a wooden two by four pole that seems to be anchoring the dock in place. When I reach the end of the rickety structure, I sit down and lean against the pole opposite her.

As I sit there, I clench my jaw in the hopes that she'll break the silence. But she doesn't.

"So…" I say with uncertainty.

"What did Mollie tell you?" she asks with a bite to the words.

"What would she tell me?" I counter.

Luna shrugs.

"Can I ask you something?" She nods. "If you don't trust her, why is she your VP?"

Luna finally looks at me and the moon reflects in her eyes, making them shimmer. For a split second, I forget why I'm here. I forget how frustrating she is, how controlling she is. For a split second, all I see is her beauty, all I see is her as a woman.

Then she opens her mouth and reality comes crashing down on me.

"Do you trust every single Soulless Kings' member?"

"With my life," I say without hesitation.

"Bullshit," she spits out.

"I don't know how it is with you and the Devil's Handmaidens, but in our club, we have each other's backs." I stretch my legs out in front of me, careful to avoid hitting her with my boot. "That's how it has to be."

"So you have it all figured out?" she scoffs.

I huff out a laugh. "I don't have shit figured out. But trust? That's a given. Once a brother is patched, they have my trust." I shrug. "Until they fucking don't."

"I learned not to trust people six years ago."

There it is, the reason we're together in this moment, the thing that binds us even though I'm not one hundred percent certain as to how. Before I address that though, the need to ease her mind about her VP sinks its claws into me.

"For the record, Mollie didn't tell me anything."

Luna gives a curt nod.

"Back there, in the house," I hitch a thumb over my shoulder. "You asked what I know about Conrad Templeton."

"What? You know more than just that he's bad news?"

I take a deep breath and push it out, expelling the last of my hesitation to tell her what I know.

"As a matter of fact…"

Luna kicks her legs out, not bothering to be careful like I was. She crosses her arms over her chest and hardens her expression. I can't help but wonder if that's her subconscious trying to put up walls, but it doesn't matter. I've gotta burn them the fuck down if we have any hope of stopping the trafficking going on so close to home.

"I know he killed my mom," she says when I don't elaborate. "I know he's at the head of some cult, and I know he's got a fucking impenetrable security team because we haven't been able to get close to him."

Admiration hits me. She knows way more than I would have guessed.

"How do you know he killed your mom?" I ask, needing to know and also hoping her response will shed some light on why she lays so much blame at my feet.

"She told me."

I arch a brow in confusion. "Care to elaborate?"

"The night he…" She swallows before taking a deep breath. "When I found her, she'd written initials in her blood."

"Okay, but initials are just that… initials. They could've belonged to anyone."

"Normally, I'd agree. But he always creeped Mom out." Luna rises to her feet and begins to pace the length of the dock. "He was demanding of her time and then there's—" Luna presses her lips together and stops pacing next to me. "Can I trust you?" she asks.

I stand up and face her, my feet braced apart. "You don't even trust your VP. I could tell you to trust me until I'm blue in the face and I'm pretty sure you won't believe me."

"Then show me I can," she snaps.

I drop my head back and stare at the sky, inhaling shaky breaths. This chick is impossible and infuriating. How the fuck am I supposed to show her she can trust me?

You know exactly how.

As soon as the thought enters my mind, I embrace it. I *do* know how.

The only problem is, showing her she can trust me has the potential to complicate things between us more than any mistrust or suspicion ever could.

CHAPTER FOURTEEN

Why? Why is this happening?

Luna

My chest heaves as I stand there, waiting for Riker to show me I can trust him. The way he's staring at the sky makes me wonder if I'm asking the impossible of him.

"Forget it."

I throw my arms in the air and turn to walk away but his strained voice halts me before I can take a step.

"What's your safe word?"

I whirl around. "What?"

Riker huffs out a breath. "Your safe word… what is it?"

"I don't…" I shake my head as if that will make his question make sense. "You've gotta be kidding?"

"Not kidding."

"But… you… I don't understand how knowing my safe word will make me trust you."

The problem is, I *do* know. I know exactly what he's

trying to do and every cell in my body wants to let him try. Well, almost every cell.

Riker reaches for my chin so fast I don't realize what he's doing until he grips it in his fingers.

"What. Is. Your. Safe. Word?" he demands.

I search his eyes, trying to find some hint that this is a joke, that he's fucking with me, but I don't find what I'm looking for. I'm not sure what I do see but it's certainly not funny.

"Luna," he prods. "Answer me."

"I don't know!" I shout as I break out of his hold.

His eyes narrow and he drops his arms to his sides. "I don't believe you."

The air around me seems to thicken and suddenly, I'm sweating. I run my fingers through my hair, lifting it off my neck to allow the night air to cool me down.

If you want him to prove you can trust him then you need to let him in. You need to show him he can trust you.

I take a deep breath and force the confession past my lips. "I haven't used a safe word in six years."

Riker's shoulders slump and he drops back a step, almost as if he was struck by a heavy weight and couldn't hold himself up.

"I don't understand," he says. "You're a submissive, right? You really haven't needed a safe word in six years? All your doms are just that good, huh?"

I could leave him with his assumptions but that doesn't feel right. Sure, it would be easier for me, less… exposing, but it would be a lie. And a lie isn't going to establish trust.

"I only use a safe word when I'm in a scene or with a dom."

"Are you…?" He scratches the back of his head. "Are you telling me you haven't been with a dom in six years?"

"Sort of," I say. "I haven't been with anyone, dom or otherwise."

He stares at me, his eyes locked on mine, questions dancing in them. When I can't stand the scrutiny any longer, I turn to walk away again.

Riker grabs my arm and spins me before tugging me toward him. I tip my head back so I can look at his face, our height difference more apparent this close. He brushes his knuckles over my cheek, under my hair, and wraps his fingers around the back of my neck.

"I used to watch you," he says. "Back when I first started going to Jacks and Jills. Did you know that?"

My eyelids flutter closed, and I force them open. "N-no."

"I remember the first time I saw you." Riker rests his other hand on my hip and electricity flows from the spot, through my veins. "You were sitting at the bar, tossing back shots of something. There was this guy, and he was trying to get your attention, but you weren't having it."

I know the night he's talking about. I remember it well because the second he walked into the club, it was as if everyone else disappeared. I remember feeling like the oxygen had been sucked out of the room. I remember seeking out the newcomer, locking my gaze on him. I remember a sense of desperation. And then I remember—

"You went straight to my mom when you arrived," I accuse, pulling away from him.

"And the first thing I asked her was your name," he says, reaching for my hand.

"Bullshit," I snap. "Why didn't she ever tell me that? She was always trying to set me up with doms… always the matchmaker. But never once did she try to set us up. If you were so drawn to me, why is that?"

Riker traces my lips with his thumb and sensations ricochet through my system, all of them familiar. Out of sheer will, I manage to stop the moan that bubbles up the back of my throat.

"What is your safe word, Luna?"

Without thinking, I give him what he wants. "Death," I breathe. "It was always 'death'."

Suddenly, Riker removes his hands and takes a step back. My eyes shoot open, and I stare at him, my chest heaving, my pussy clenching. Something flashes in his irises, but I can't identify it. Shock, maybe? Disbelief? Whatever it is, it disappears so quickly I convince myself it was a figment of my imagination.

"Do you have any weapons on you?" he asks.

"Of course," I scoff.

Riker holds out his hand. "Give them to me."

"No."

He leans forward until I can feel his breath skate across my skin. "I don't tolerate disobedience," he snarls and wraps his fingers around a thick lock of hair to tug my head back. "Give them to me."

The sting in my scalp travels through my head, down my body, and seems to settle between my thighs in a delicious flood of lust. As if under a spell, I bend to retrieve the knife in my left boot and then the one in the right. Riker's hold loosens as I do, and I hand him both blades.

He grabs them and tosses one to the dock without breaking eye contact. "Anything else?" he asks with a quirked brow.

I reach behind me and grab the pistol out of my waistband. I hand it to him but don't release it easily. He must sense how hard it is for me to part with it and doesn't push. Instead, he simply stands there, his nostrils flaring, his stare unyielding, and waits me out. When I finally let go, he grins.

"Thank you."

I nod.

"Take off your cut," Riker commands as he sets the gun with the discarded knife.

"No."

He points the knife he's still holding at my chest, the tip pressing against my flesh above the neckline of my shirt. Dragging it downward, he exposes the top of my lace bra.

"Take. It. Off," he growls.

My safe word is on the tip of my tongue.

Death. Death. Death.

Submitting to someone is one thing but giving up an item that is so key to my identity, that's another. Yet, I don't utter the word. Instead, I push myself past my comfort zone and shrug out of the leather.

Before it can fall to the ground, Riker grabs it and turns away from me to hang it on one of the poles at the end of the dock. I watch as he takes his own cut off and hangs it with mine, shoving my knife in the pocket. His muscles bunch and ripple and I step toward him with my arms stretched out.

"Did I say you could touch me?" he asks.

I quickly yank my hands back and lower my head. "No, sir."

I focus my stare on his boots and when he comes back to me, his fingers graze my chin, and he lifts my head.

"Do you want to touch me?"

His voice curls around me like a warm blanket on a winter night. I soak up the heat and let it fuel my response.

"More than I should."

"Excuse me?" he growls.

"Oh, um… yes, sir."

Why does this man have me so tongue-tied?

Riker holds his hand out, palm up. "Give me your hand."

I lay my hand on top of his and his fingertips graze my skin. The contact tickles but he quickly moves his fingers to my wrist, wrapping them around me. When he pulls my hand toward his chest, I tense up.

"Trust," he whispers. "All you have to do is use your safe word if you're uncomfortable."

I nod as I try to swallow but it's almost impossible with how dry my mouth is.

Riker flattens my hand over his pec and flexes. When the muscles jump under my touch, my fingers automatically curl into his flesh. Next, he grabs my other hand and guides them both down his stomach, bringing them to rest just above the button of his jeans. The entire time, his eyes are locked on mine, holding my stare hostage.

"Take them off."

I suck in a breath at the command but no matter how hard I try, my brain can't get my fingers to cooperate. I silently wait for the punishment that should come for disobeying his order, but Riker surprises me.

Instead of making another demand, he roughly grabs my hips and yanks me forward so my body collides with his. He quickly unbuttons my jeans and drags them, along with my panties, down my legs, crouching as he does.

I'm exposed to him, vulnerable in a way I haven't let myself be in years. When his hands shift to my ass and he squeezes, my head falls back on a moan. Fuck, it's been too long since someone touched me.

Riker leans forward and buries his face between my thighs. He inhales my scent and my legs quiver from the sensation.

"Spread your legs," he demands from his position, and I do as he says.

When his tongue darts out and swirls around my clit, a shiver races down my spine. Without thinking, I brace myself using his head, yanking his hair in response to his erotic torture.

Riker grows, the rumble low and vibrating. He laps at me, sucks my clit into his mouth and flicks it with his tongue.

"You taste like honey mixed with sunshine," he groans, the movement of his lips acting like a match setting fire to my body.

Of their own volition, my hips move, undulating toward him like an alcoholic on the street begging for change to buy his next drink. But unlike that alcoholic, I've refrained from my vice for so long that any little taste sends me into drunken oblivion.

Riker moves his hand to the back of my thigh and lifts my leg to guide it over his shoulder, opening me up more for him. He ravages me, assaults my pussy, and my senses, until I explode. Lights dance behind my tightly closed eyelids as I spiral, spin out of control like I'm being flung through a vortex into another dimension.

When the vortex spits me out, slings me back to earth, my body doesn't stop trembling. Riker maintains a hold on me as he pulls away and rises to his feet. My eyes flutter open in time to see him lick his lips, the grin on his face making it evident that he enjoyed eating me as a middle-of-the-night snack.

Riker lifts his hand to my cheek, and I lean into his palm. "You coming undone for me… priceless," he says.

"Mmmm."

"But we're not done."

"We're not?"

"Not even fucking close."

Wrapping his hand around the back of my neck, he drags me toward him and fuses his mouth with mine. He thrusts his tongue past my lips, the tip touching mine. There's nothing tentative or sweet about the kiss. It's primal, demanding, incredibly fevered.

Riker lifts me off the dock and I wrap my legs around his

waist, my core settling against his bare skin. I'm dimly aware of him carrying me, of his footsteps echoing in the dark on the wooden structure. When he steps off into the grass, he lowers me to the ground, never once breaking the kiss.

He cups my tit with one hand and reaches beneath me to unclasp my bra with the other. Riker pulls the lacy garment off me and tosses it to the side. He moves his hand from my chest, down my stomach until he reaches his own jeans. I feel his fingers working to unbutton them and when they finally come undone, he groans.

"Touch me," he breathes after breaking the kiss and then he slowly shifts his mouth to my nipple.

I reach between our bodies, seeking out his rigid cock. When I grip him in my hand, his body jerks and he bites down. The pain is brief before it morphs into something else, something hot and delicious.

"Ah, fuck," he moans.

My hand is scraping against his zipper as I pump his dick, but I don't care. I'd rub my hands raw before I stop this. In the next instant, Riker's weight disappears as he shifts to his knees and then his feet. I watch him shove his pants and boxer briefs down his legs, kicking them off with his boots.

Holy. Fucking. Shit.

Riker is ripped, a perfect display of muscle and ink and power and... man. His body is corded in a way I could only dream about and even then, my wildest dreams wouldn't do him justice.

"Luna, I'm gonna need you to stop touching that pussy," he snarls, staring down at me. "It's mine."

His words snap me back to reality and I realize my hand is between my thighs, rubbing fast circles over my clit. My knees are bent and spread wide open, begging him to wedge between them. Feeling defiant, and on the brink of another trip through the vortex, I don't stop.

Riker narrows his eyes. "I'm warning you, Luna. You're playing with fire."

I lift my lips into a sultry smile as I use my free hand to pinch my nipple. "Come burn with me."

In a move so fast I don't have time to react, Riker flips me onto my stomach and drops to his knees in the grass next to me. He holds me in place by resting his forearm across my back and bends so I can feel his ragged breathing near my ear.

"I warned you."

He removes his arm from my back and before I realize what's happening, his palm connects with my bare ass cheeks. Riker quickly rubs over the area to ease the sting. Pleasure ripples through me, and I curl my fingers in the grass.

His hand disappears.

"Don't ever disobey me."

Slap.

Slap.

Slap.

Every time he spanks me, my hips jerk forward, seeking contact with anything it can to increase the pleasure.

"If I have to tell you again…"

Slap.

Rather than rubbing the sting away, he reaches between my legs and shoves a finger inside me, crooking it to hit that magical spot.

"… I'll fuck this pussy until there's no doubt who it belongs to." He pulls his finger out and rolls me to my back. "Understand?"

I nod, unable to form words.

"I can't hear you."

"Yes, sir," I whimper.

"Good girl." Riker positions himself above me. "I'm gonna take what's mine now, my love."

Those two words, uttered so perfectly, send a wave of panic crashing over my body, dousing the flames he's ignited. My breath hitches and my muscles tense. Riker freezes, sensing the shift and stares at me.

"You've got your safe word, Luna," he reminds me. "Use it if you need to."

Why? Why is this happening?

"Luna?" Riker cups my cheek. "Say the word. It's okay."

"D-death."

CHAPTER FIFTEEN

There it is. The accusations, the blame, the anguish and suspicion.

Riker

Death.

Safe words. They're a must in any scene, any relationship or encounter within the kink community. And the moment they're said, whether mumbled a bit incoherently or shouted to the rooftops, time stops. Actions grind to a halt and the focus shifts to making sure the person using their safe word is okay.

Death.

As far as safe words go, it's a good one. The best. Because the second Luna said 'death', any pleasure I was getting from giving her so much disappeared. And, despite the protests of my dick and the severe case of blue balls I'm contending with, that's okay.

Death.

The best safe word I've ever heard. And more common than most would think.

"I'm sorry."

I glance down at Luna, who has yet to stand up. I reach a hand out and after a momentary hesitation, she grabs it and lets me help her to her feet. I tug her naked body toward me, wrapping my arms around her when she settles against my chest.

"You have nothing to be sorry for," I tell her. "I told you, if you felt uncomfortable you need to use your safe word. You were uncomfortable and used it. That's exactly what should have happened."

"But y—"

I grip her upper arms and push her back a bit so I can look her in the eyes.

"No buts, Luna," I snap. "Shit, you run a BDSM club. You know the rules, how things work." I drop my arms. "Would you tell another sub to apologize for using their safe word?"

"No."

"Exactly." I shove my fingers through my hair and heave a sigh. "I don't care that I had to stop. That's my job… make sure you're okay, *always*, and if you're not, I fix it. It's that simple."

"And that complicated," she mumbles.

I can't stop the chuckle that escapes. "Yeah, sometimes." I lift her hand in mine. "C'mon. I need you to get your clothes on before I forget all the rules."

Luna lets me dress her, both of us quiet, pensive. I wish I could read her mind, know exactly what is going on behind those sad eyes, behind that beautiful, sassy face. But I can't. In my own head, I continuously replay every second from the moment I sat next to her on the dock, trying to figure out what went wrong. I don't care that she stopped, but whatever the cause was, I need to know so I don't do it again.

Because there will be an again. Many if I have anything to say about it. The moment she put her trust in me, let herself submit, she became mine. Could I do the same with another sub? Sure, but it wouldn't be the same, would it? Because it wouldn't be Luna.

What the fuck is happening to me?

When we're both dressed, we walk side by side back toward the house. As we reach the garage, Luna stops and grabs my arm to stop me.

"What's wrong?" I ask and I look at our surroundings, wondering if she sensed something or saw something I missed.

"Don't you want to know why I said my safe word?"

Fuck yes, I do!

I shrug. "If you want to tell me, you can." I shove my hands in my pockets to stop myself from reaching out to touch her. "But it won't change anything. I will always stop if you say it."

Luna bites her lip, and the action is sexy as hell. She averts her gaze for a moment and when she returns her stare to me, she takes a deep breath.

"My mom used to call me 'my love'," she tells me, her voice barely above a whisper. "When you said that, it just… I don't know." Luna shrugs. "Pulled me out of the moment I guess."

That is not at all what I was expecting. But it makes sense. I wouldn't want anything to remind me of my parents when I'm about to fuck someone. I mentally wince, careful not to let any reaction slip into my expression.

"I'm sorry."

"Why? You didn't do anything wrong," she assures me. "Not really."

Unable to hold back any longer, I pull my hand from my pocket and tuck an errant strand of hair behind her ear.

"Is there something you'd rather I call you?"

"Luna works," she says with a cheeky grin. "Looney Tunes is also good."

"I'm not calling you Looney Tunes in the middle of sex."

She shrugs one shoulder. "Up to you."

My only response is to shake my head. I don't know what to make of her. One minute she's slinging accusations and the next she's putty in my hands. Two minutes after that, she's being playful and drawing me in like a moth to a flame.

I would do well to remember that, at the start of the night, she hated me. She's hated me for a long fucking time.

And that's why you're here. Because she hates you, not because she wants to submit to you.

Reigning in my thoughts, I refocus on the reason I wanted to dominate her in the first place. I grab ahold of why I'm even at this place.

"So, do you trust me?" I ask.

Her smile falters and she seems to ponder the question for a second before nodding.

"Yeah, I guess I do," she says.

"Good."

I urge her to continue walking and we enter the garage, stopping next to our Harleys. I straddle mine and grip the handlebars.

"What were you going to tell me before… well, before?" I ask. "You started to say something about how you knew Templeton killed Delia but then you clammed up."

Luna averts her gaze and takes a deep breath. After blowing it out, she says, "I overheard a conversation between the two of them. It was a few weeks before he killed her. I didn't catch it all but the jist of it seemed to be able him wanting to use the club to funnel victims for his trafficking ring."

"Jesus, I bet she hated that."

"Ya think?" Luna scoffs. "My mom had no problem doing

whatever it took to forge partnerships with criminals, if the endgame served her agenda. But trafficking? No way was she going to let that fly."

"Do you have any idea what happened to make him snap and kill her?"

"No." Luna shuffles her feet. "But for a long time… until tonight really, I thought you had something to do with it."

"Yeah, I got that when you were yelling at me in the house earlier," I tell her. "And now what do you think?"

I'm sure I haven't done anything specific to make her think otherwise but for whatever reason, she's changed her mind. She already said that. But why?

"Honestly?" I nod. "I think a part of me always knew you had nothing to do with it. I'd seen you and my mom together and she always talked highly of you. And then tonight, the way you were with Slim—sorry, Kenny—the way you were with him, and me…" She shrugs. "For so long, I held onto the fact that you—"

Luna presses her lips together and for a moment, I fear she's reverting back to the unfettered rage she always seemed to have toward me.

"Luna, what? What did you hold on to?"

"You were there, Riker," she cries, taking a step toward me until she's within reach. "That night, you were at the club. How did you not hear anything?"

There it is. The accusations, the blame, the anguish and suspicion.

"You're right," I agree. "I was there that day. But I was in a private room and so was she when I left. The soundproofing…" I rub my palms over my thighs in an effort not to touch her, frustrated at the memory. "I thought she was safe, doing her thing, ya know? I had no reason to think she was in danger. So I left."

Tears shimmer in Luna's eyes. "She wasn't safe."

"No shit," I snap. "But it's not my fault."

Luna throws her hands in the air. "I fucking know that!"

"Then why can't you let it go?" I ask, genuinely confused as to why her tone and her actions don't match her words. "Why do you keep circling back to the fact that I was in the club that day?"

Luna begins to pace the length of the garage. After a few minutes of tense silence, I start my Harley. I need to get out of here, away from her and her pain. I glance at her one last time, and she refuses to look at me.

Without a second thought, I pull out of the garage and drive around to the front of the house, opening up the throttle when I hit the road.

Fuck Luna McAllister and her Looney Tunes ways.

CHAPTER SIXTEEN

Nothing changed.

Luna

"Are you really gonna just let him go?"

I whirl around and see Mollie standing in the doorway leading from the garage to the kitchen. She's leaning against the frame, her arms crossed over her chest. I notice she's changed into sweats, no doubt trying to settle in for the night and get some rest while she can.

"What choice do I have?"

I cross the space to enter the house, but she blocks my path.

"There's always a choice, Looney Tunes," Mollie says softly. "And ever since your mom, you seem to be making a lot of the wrong ones."

"What's that supposed to mean?" I snap, pissed off that she knows me so well.

"It means whatever you need it to mean."

With that, she turns and disappears into the house. The

lock clicks and I punch the door. How dare she lock me out? I own this house. Fuck, I own her.

No, you don't. You're not like Templeton. You don't own *people.*

"Motherfucker!" I shout into the silence.

I get on my Harley and the second the engine fires, I tear out of the garage. I turn onto the quiet street and head in the direction I know Riker went. It's the only direction he could go, with the road being a dead end.

I push the bike as hard as I can, doing my best to catch up to him. When I reach a red light, I reluctantly brake to a stop. Swiveling my head in both directions, I see no other vehicles. I could run the light and would probably be fine but why chance it?

The light turns green, and I gun the engine. After the next block, I come to the interstate and have a decision to make: head east, toward the coast in the hopes that Riker is going home to the Soulless Kings property, or head toward Jacks and Jills, scouring the streets for him on the off chance he's staying in Portland.

I drive onto the interstate and watch my speedometer climb. Sixty miles per hour, seventy, eighty, eighty-five, ninety-two, ninety-six. I level out there, praying I'll catch up to Riker and can stop this ridiculous one-sided chase.

Seven miles pass and that's when I see the motorcycle up ahead. I focus on the small taillight and when I'm able, I swerve to pull up next to him. Riker quickly looks at me and even in the dark, I can see his eyes narrow. Hell, I'm sure I'd see steam billowing from his ears if I looked hard enough.

Riker doesn't slow down. Instead, he maintains his speed, which is okay because it's not the ninety-six I was going to catch him. I slow down even more and weave back to follow behind him rather than stay next to him.

We ride like this for another half hour and when he takes

his exit, the sun is peeking over the horizon to join the moon before they both go their respective ways for the day. Maybe I should take a page from their book and leave Riker alone, go home and take care of business.

I dismiss the idea as quickly as it came. I followed him for a reason, even if that reason has yet to reveal itself to me.

As I continue to follow Riker, I let myself enjoy the ride, the wind, and salty ocean air. I don't get to the coast often and while this isn't a pleasure cruise, that doesn't mean I can't soak up something good.

Riker weaves down back roads, expertly navigating the curves. When he comes up on a stop sign, he flips his signal on and turns left, without bothering to stop. I do the same.

Another mile goes by, and he slows his Harley, swerving to the right and coming to a stop in front of a closed gate. He lowers the kickstand and jumps off his bike before turning and stalking toward me.

"What the fuck are you doing?" he shouts when I cut the engine.

"Taking a leisurely ride," I reply with a bite to my tone. "You?"

Before he can yell at me some more, a figure appears on the other side of the gate.

"Ah, Riker," the guy calls. "Everything okay?"

"Do I look okay to you, Royal?" Riker snaps in response.

"You look like you're being chased by a crazy bitch."

I charge the gate, pulling out my pistol and pointing it through the bars at his head. "What the fuck did you just call me?" I snarl at him.

"Yep. Crazy bitch fits."

Riker wraps his arms around me from behind and pushes my arm down. I try to maintain my stance but even I have to admit he's much stronger than me. And that only serves to piss me off even more.

"Royal, shut the fuck up before you get yourself shot." Riker spins me around. "Luna, why the hell did you follow me?"

"I swear to God, Riker, if your boy doesn't quit staring at my ass, I'm gonna kill him."

Riker looks past me at Royal and a growl barrels out of him. He steps around me and I turn in time to see him rattle the gate.

"Open the gate, Royal."

Royal's eyes dart from Riker to me and back again. He heaves a sigh and turns to go back to the gatehouse. In the next instant, the gate is swinging open, and Riker is through the opening the second he can fit.

Riker launches himself at Royal, taking him to the ground. He hauls his arm back and lands a punch to Royal's face, sending blood squirting from the guy's nose.

"What the hell, Riker?" Royal cries, bringing his hands up to cup his face.

"If you ever look at her like that again, she won't have to worry about killing you because I'll end you myself," Riker snarls. "Got it?"

"Yes!"

"She's not some crazy bitch or Bangin' Betty. She's fucking mine."

"Do I get a say in that?" I ask, walking to stand next to them.

If I'm being honest with myself, I don't care that I don't have a say. At least not at this moment. Because watching Riker defend me, get possessive and jealous? That alone makes me following him worth it.

Riker shoves himself off Royal and stands. His chest is heaving, and his eyes are wild, but he's focused on me. His fists are clenched at his sides, but he starts flexing them, almost as if he's trying to flex the anger away.

"Don't interrupt me when I'm dealing with a prospect again."

My brows shoot up. "Don't treat me like I'm one of your pathetic minions you can boss around." I lift my gun and press the barrel against his chest. "I'm not a Soulless King. If you want to claim me, fine, but you will treat me with respect and like the goddamn queen I am."

Riker seems to think about that for a minute before nodding. "Deal."

I drop my arm. "Fucking hell you're gonna be the death of me."

"Uh, guys," Royal interrupts and Riker looks over his shoulder at him. "If you're done with whatever..." He sweeps his arm at us. "Well, whatever the hell this is, can I get back to work?"

Riker turns and extends a hand to help Royal to his feet. The prospect dusts himself off and returns to the little hut and plops into the chair. Riker and I return to our bikes and drive them through so the gates can be closed. Before we leave Royal, Riker gets one last dig in.

"Don't make me regret not beating the shit out of you."

With that, Riker guns his engine and I follow down the winding gravel road until we reach a clearing. A large structure looms before us and I realize we've reached the clubhouse.

Finally.

"Sorry about that," Riker says after parking. "Royal's a good kid but he still has a bit to learn."

"It's fine." He eyes me skeptically. "Really, it is. I know what prospects are like. And if you think yours are bad, try dealing with all female prospects."

Riker chuckles and the tension is broken. "No thanks. Women are complicated enough without adding in the pressure prospecting brings."

A door creaks, pulling my attention to the porch on the clubhouse. A tall man steps out and a petite woman follows him, tucking herself into his side when they stop at the top of the steps.

"Riker, you pulled us out of bed early for a reason," he says, sounding angry. "Either get your ass inside and fill us in or I'm gonna let Charlie do her worst."

"You're messing with my morning… *routine*," the woman says. "And trust me, you don't want that."

"I thought the sex stopped after the vows," Riker jokes.

"I don't know why you'd think that. It just keeps getting better."

The man lifts the woman, and she wraps her legs around his waist as she fuses her lips to his. I know I should look away but damn. I don't want to.

"Fuck, that's enough," Riker laughs and grabs my hand to drag me toward the steps. He pushes past the couple and looks at me. "That's Fender," he says and raises his voice. "Our ruthless Prez."

Fender sets the woman on her feet and swipes at his mouth. He laughs and focuses on Riker and me. "And this is Charlie, my ol' lady." He wraps his arm around her shoulders and pulls her close.

I extend my hand. "Luna," I say. "President of Devil's Handmaidens MC."

"Damn, bro." Fender whistles. "You're way out of your league."

"Stop," Charlie says and smacks Fender on the chest. She turns feisty eyes to Riker. "I'm sure he already knows that."

The banter between the couple and Riker is infectious. It's clear they all love one another, that they're a family. This is how it is within my club so I know how that feels, what it's like to know that no matter what, the people you're surrounded by will always be there.

"Let's just go inside," Riker snaps.

I glance at him out of the corner of my eye, trying to gauge if he's actually upset, but the grin he's trying to hide is a dead giveaway. He's loving every second of this.

We all walk into the clubhouse, and I'm struck with a sense of familiarity. Nothing looks the same as the DHMC clubhouse but the feeling of it, the vibe the space gives off is the same.

Within seconds, we're surrounded by club members, all wearing cuts and dressed as if they're ready for anything. It's impressive considering the early morning hour and knowing exactly how hard MCs tend to party, regardless of what day of the week it is.

"What's going on?" another man asks Riker and a quick glance at his patch tells me he's the VP.

"Piston, this is Luna," Riker says rather than answering the question. "Luna, this is Piston, VP and all-around asshole."

"Dude, it's the fucking ass crack of dawn," Piston says with aggravation. "I'm tired."

"Nice to meet you," I say, hoping to tone down the frustration.

"You too," Piston says, smiling slightly. "Why are you here?"

Riker reacts as quickly to Piston as he did with Royal and grabs the VP by his cut.

"I figured Holland would've taught you better manners by now," Riker snarls.

Rather than fight back, Piston rolls his eyes. "She's tried. Says there's no hope."

"Look," I interject. "If it's an issue for me to be here, I can go."

"No," Riker says over his shoulder. "You followed me here so you're staying."

"Why did you follow him exactly?" another member asks from behind Piston.

"Aw, fuck, Joker," Riker groans. "Not you too."

"What?" Joker shrugs. "Last I heard, she hated you. Can you blame me for wondering what changed?"

"Yeah, I—"

"Nothing changed," I say, interrupting Riker. All eyes turn to me. "Okay, maybe something has changed but what exactly that is, is none of your fucking business." I push past them all and walk farther into the room like I own the place, calling over my shoulder as I do.

"Are we gonna meet about Templeton or what?"

CHAPTER SEVENTEEN

I really don't want to have to bury his body because he's following my orders.

Riker

"Another one bites the dust."

I don't take my eyes off the sway of Luna's hips as she walks away from me and my brothers. Her ass cheeks are perfectly sculpted in the dark wash jeans and my mouth is watering from the sight alone.

"Dude, you're so fucked, and you don't even know it."

When a pair of lips hit my cheek, I'm pulled out of my trance. I turn to see Charlie, her grin so big it would split her face if it could.

"What did you say?" I ask.

"Yep," she laughs. "Fucked for sure."

"Babe, leave him alone," Fender says with zero force in the words.

There was a time that seeing the two of them together would send the whole of Soulless Kings into a frenzy but now, it's normal… and weird when they aren't together.

"Are you coming or not?" Luna calls again and when I look in her direction, I see she's stopped with her arms crossed over her chest and a bored expression on her face.

"I like her," Joker says as he slaps me on the back and scurries to join Luna.

"Yeah, me too," I mutter.

"Hey, bro?"

I turn to the left and see Trainwreck walking toward me. He's got a focused look on his face, one that reminds me why I texted Fender to call emergency church when I was stopped at that red light.

"What's up?" I ask him when he stops in front of me.

"Did she give you anything?"

"Excuse me?"

"Luna," he says. "What did she tell you about Templeton?"

"Ah, right." I shake my head, annoyed that my mind immediately went to what took place on that dock instead of the obvious reason Trainwreck asked the question. "Not much more than we already know." I clap him on the back. "Let's get into church and we can all go over it together."

Trainwreck takes off so fast one would think a fire was lit under his ass. He's so focused on Templeton, on doing whatever it takes to stop the people responsible for his sister's kidnapping, that he seems to have forgotten how to relax. I get it but he needs to find that balance between the good and evil in the world. Otherwise, he won't survive much longer.

Like you found the balance tonight?

I stride across the room and turn down the hall toward the meeting room. When I step through the doorway, I take out my weapons and drop them in the box. Luna's weapons catch my eye, and I can't stop the upward tug of my lips. So, the redheaded vixen knows how to pick her battles.

Piston bangs the gavel on the table, and everyone sits down in their usual places… everyone except Luna. She steps up next to Fender at the head of the table and looks around the room.

"What?" she snaps when no one says anything as they stare at her.

"This isn't your show, sweetheart," Gibson says.

Luna's eyes widen and she stalks toward Gibson's chair. When she steps up behind him, she wraps her fingers around the back of his neck.

"It's Luna," she seethes. "Or Looney Tunes. But never 'sweetheart.'"

"Please tell me you're gonna lock shit down with her, Riker," Squirrel jokes, a glint of humor in his eyes.

Luna turns to him and if looks were a vehicle, Squirrel would be roadkill. He lifts his hands in surrender.

"Sorry," he says quickly.

Luna grins and returns to stand next to Fender's seat. "It's fine."

"At the risk of inviting your wrath," Fender begins and stands up. "I know you're an MC president and are used to calling the shots. But here, on my turf, I'm in charge. If you overstep again, touch my men again, you'll be banned from the property, relationship with a brother or not. Understood?"

It takes every fiber of my being not to jump out of my chair and launch myself at Fender for how he's speaking to Luna, but I manage. Girlfriends are not permitted in this room. Neither are ol' ladies and Luna is neither.

Right?

Regardless of what label our connection gives her, she needs to understand that this isn't the DHMC. This is Soulless Kings' territory, and she has no power here. Fortunately for me, Fender has no problem putting anyone in their place so I don't have to. Luna's a bit… well, let's just say she's earned her road name fair and square and I'm not about to be the one to invoke that side of her.

"Understood," she finally answers. "And I'm sorry. It's a habit that's hard to break."

"Break it," Fender barks. "Fast."

"Look," Luna begins and scans the room. "I know I hold no power here. But the fact of the matter is, you're going to need me and my club, both my clubs. You have no idea what you're up against when it comes to Templeton."

"We have some idea," Squirrel states.

He quickly pulls out his laptop and connects it to the projector.

"What're you doing?" Luna asks.

"Just wait, swee—" Luna glares at Gibson and he corrects himself. "Sorry. Just wait… *Looney Tunes*."

"Better," Luna says on a laugh.

The projector lights up and the websites that Squirrel pulled up during our last church appear on the screen.

"As you can see, we know quite a bit," Fender says to Luna.

Luna turns to look at the screen and her sharp intake of breath reaches my ears through the tense room. She reaches behind her and grips the edge of the table, and her knuckles turn white.

"Holy shit," she mumbles.

"Add this to what you told me earlier," I say as I stand and walk toward her. "We should be able to come up with a plan to take him down."

"What did you tell him earlier?" Trainwreck demands.

"We'll get to that," I bark at him. "Give her—"

"Hey, check this out," Squirrel says, expanding one of the tabs on his laptop so it's the only one we see on the screen.

I read the news article headline: Billionaire Follows Promising Lead to Find Missing Daughter.

"I don't know if this is good or bad," I admit.

"Why?" Fender asks.

"Templeton's a fucking monster," I say, facing him. "If he's following a lead, on one hand, I hope that means she's alive. On the other hand, I hate that she'll end up back with him."

"I get it," he agrees and shifts his attention to Luna. "Hey, you okay?"

I glance at her and notice her face has drained of color. She's shaking her head and her lips are silently moving as she reads the full article.

"I, uh…" Luna looks at me with an expression I can't discern. "I'm sorry." She races toward the door. "I gotta go."

"Luna, wait," I say, rushing behind her.

"Riker, I can't," she bends to rifle through the box of weapons.

Fortunately, she was the first person in the room so they're at the bottom. I grab her arm to stop her from leaving.

"Talk to me," I demand. "What is going on?"

"If Templeton has a lead on his daughter…" Her face hardens and she heaves a sigh. "Paulina Templeton is at a DHMC safe house."

I wasn't expecting that.

Luna yanks out of my hold and races down the hall. Her admission stuns me but when several brothers push past me, I snap out of it.

I run down the hall and out the front door, just in time to see Luna riding away on her Harley. I yank my phone out of my pocket and dial Royal's number.

"Yo," he answers on the second ring.

"Lock it down," I bark into the phone. "Luna's headed your way. Don't let her leave."

"Ah, Riker," he says. "She doesn't like me too much."

"I don't give a flying fuck if she tries to kill you," I shout. I throw my leg over the seat of my bike. "She doesn't get off the property."

I disconnect the call and drive like a bat out of hell toward the gate. It's not like Luna has a huge head start but Royal is right, Luna is not his biggest fan. And I really don't want to have to bury his body because he's following *my* orders.

CHAPTER EIGHTEEN

I need your help.

Luna

"I'm under strict orders."

I dismount my Harley and stalk toward Royal, knife in hand and blade ready. He lifts his hands in a gesture of surrender, as if that's going to stop me from chopping him into tiny little pieces and scattering them on the highway once I get the fuck out of here.

"Royal, open the goddamn gate," I order him.

A motorcycle engine pulls my focus away from the prospect and I whirl around to see Riker braking to a stop.

"Luna, put the damn knife away," he barks.

"I don't fucking think so!" I shout. "I need to get to the safe house."

The rumble of Harley's echoes through the air and the ground trembles seconds before a pack of bikers comes into view. I can't take my eyes off of them as they exit the property. I glance over my shoulder and see Royal standing at the gatehouse, a grin on his face as he pulls his hand away from the button that opens the gate.

Royal shrugs. "Sorry. I take orders from them, not you."

"Call Mollie and let her know the Soulless Kings are on their way. Then text me the address of all your safe houses and the DHMC clubhouse so I can forward it to Fender and Greaser."

Riker stands there after issuing his demand looking like the cat that ate the fucking canary. I know he's trying to help but I don't need it. I don't need him.

"You're crossing a line, Riker," I tell him. "I may not get to call the shots in there." I stab a finger in the direction of his clubhouse. "And I may let you order me around in the bedroom, but when it comes to my club, the people we help, I don't submit to anyone."

Royal whistles and I turn to lunge at him. Riker's arms come around my stomach to hold me back.

"Let me go, Riker," I demand, struggling to get out of his arms.

"Not until you calm down and see reason."

"Are you fucking calling me crazy?!"

Riker heaves a sigh and loosens his grip. He doesn't let go but he doesn't relax a little.

"Your own club named you Looney Tunes," he reminds me. "Judging by your actions, they weren't far off."

"Fuck you."

Riker leans in close to my ear and whispers, "We'll get to that, I promise you. But right now, I need you to calm the fuck down and listen to me. I'm trying to help you, not step on your toes."

Without letting me go, Riker reaches into my pocket and pulls out my cell phone. He shoves it in my face.

"Call Mollie," he says. "Now."

I snatch the phone from him and when Riker drops his arms, I whirl around and glare.

"Don't ev—"

"Call. Mollie." He enunciates the words, and his tone leaves no more room for argument.

I walk a few feet away while I hit the speed dial button for my VP and put the cell to my ear. Mollie answers on the third ring and I can tell by her almost unintelligible words that I woke her up.

"You're about to get company," I say by way of greeting.

"What?" she mumbles and an image of her sitting up in bed and rubbing her eyes hits me. "Who?"

"Get your ass out of bed and alert the other safe houses, as well as anyone at the clubhouse."

"What are you talking about?" she asks again, more alert.

I glance over my shoulder and Riker and see him talking in hushed tones to Royal. I heave a sigh and refocus on my conversation with Mollie.

"Soulless Kings. They just headed out and I don't want them showing up to surprise anyone."

"Luna, what's going on? Why the hell would Sou—"

"Just fucking do it," I snap.

"Yeah, okay." The line becomes muffled, as if she's changing and the clothes are dragging across the microphone in her cell. "I'll call the other safe houses and Spooks at the clubhouse. What about Jacks and Jills? Do we need to be on alert there?"

"It wouldn't hurt," I tell her, annoyed I didn't think of that. "Listen, I'm sure everything is fine, and the Soulless Kings are overreacting but there was a news piece about Templeton having a lead on his *missing daughter's* whereabouts. I'm sure you can imagine that would be horrible considering *we* have her."

"Do you think he really knows where she is or is he just blowing smoke?"

I shrug and then remember she can't see me. "I don't know. But I don't want to take any chances."

"Right. Got it."

I slowly make my way back to Riker while I end my call with Mollie.

"Just let everyone know what's going on," I reiterate. "Not Paulina or any of the victims though. I don't want to scare them. Riker and I are going to head to the clubhouse and tell everyone to head that way once the Soulless Kings do whatever it is they're going to do to make sure all our locations are not exposed in any way."

Riker ends his conversation with Royal and steps up close to me.

"Okay. See you soon," she says.

"Be careful and be prepared for anything," I tell Mollie.

"Always."

I disconnect the call and then send a text to Riker with all of the pertinent addresses. He takes a moment and forwards them to Fender and Greaser. No doubt the second they can pull over, they will so they can figure out who's going to what location. It's what I'd do, what DHMC would do.

"Thank you," Riker says and cups my cheek. "I know this isn't easy for you but remember, it's not about you. If you keep that in mind, it won't feel so bad."

"Riker, you need to understand something." I grab his wrist and lower his arm. "I can and will do whatever it takes to keep safe those I want to protect. I have no problem with that. What I do have a problem with is someone trying to take over because they think they can do it better than me."

He falls back a step. "Is that what you think? That we have some fucked up notion that we're better?"

"Of course you do." I tilt my head. "That's what men do.

They think they can do everything better than a woman. But I'm not just any chick. I will fucking burn someone's world down and stand there holding the gas can and match with a smile on my face."

"I don't doubt that for a second," he insists. "But even you have to admit that two gas cans are better than one." He squares his shoulders. "Let me ask you something."

"What?"

"If a victim of Templeton came to you and asked if they could help you take him down, would you put up this big of a fight?"

Riker's question throws me for a second because I've never thought about that. There has never been a victim who has asked to help. They've begged for safety, for *our* help, but never offered their own.

"That depends," I say honestly.

"On what?"

"On whether or not the person would actually be of some help or if their help would only hinder. Not everyone can do what we do."

"You're right, they can't," he says. "But you have people who can help in a big way, and they aren't doing it for you. Hell, they're not even trying to tell you to back off and let them handle it. All they're doing is trying to get justice for one of their own."

"I'm not following."

Riker heaves a sigh and steps around me to go to his Harley. I follow his lead and do the same while I wait for him to elaborate.

"The Soulless Kings have beef with Conrad Templeton," he says. Riker's face hardens and the veins in his neck bulge from anger. "He's responsible for the kidnapping of Trainwreck's twin when they were nine. She managed to escape when she was twenty-one but not before the damage was done. She's married to Greaser, our road captain, and they have a son now. She's doing great and her abductors are in prison, but Templeton isn't. And it all happened because he lies to people, convinces them that what they're doing is somehow going to get them closer to him and to a better afterlife. It's fucking nuts and we need him to pay."

My body vibrates with rage. How in the hell did I miss this? In all the years I've been chasing him, how did I not know about the connection to the Soulless Kings? How have we not crossed paths before since both clubs are chasing the same villain?

"I'm sorry."

The words seem inadequate, but they're all I've got.

"Don't be sorry," Riker says. "Just stop trying to control the situation and accept the fact that you aren't the only person who needs this. We all do."

"I… you're right."

Images of my mom lying on the club floor in a pool of her blood, of every person who's shown up at Jacks and Jills for help… they all flash through my mind like I'm flipping through a scrapbook of my worst memories. All the sleepless nights, the research, the endless number of hours wasted on trying to track down Templeton… it all comes flooding back.

And it all makes me more determined than ever to find him and kill him.

"Riker," I say and lock eyes with him. "The DHMC needs your help, your club's help." I swallow past the lump in my throat. "*I* need your help."

He stares at me for a long moment, almost as if he's trying to figure out whether or not I'm serious. Finally, he nods and fires up his Harley.

"Let's ride."

CHAPTER NINETEEN

Looney Tunes, the Nightmare Room is going to be your new favorite playground.

Riker

"Why did you bring her here?"

Luna's shout across the DHMC clubhouse pulls my attention from my brothers. I blow out the smoke from the joint I just hit and pass it to Fender before turning to see her stride toward the door. Her face is pinched, and her fists are clenched at her sides.

"She looks pissed," Piston comments.

"That's because she is." I nod toward the two people who just entered the clubhouse, the ones on the receiving end of Luna's wrath, and narrow my eyes. "Isn't that Templeton's daughter?"

Squirrel yanks out his phone and pulls up the two news articles on the girl's disappearance. He shoves the device in front of my face, and I stare at the pictures that are included with the reports. Sure enough, there's my confirmation. One of Luna's sisters brought the girl here when they were expressly told not to.

"You might want to go see what's going on," Fender says as he claps my back. He hands me the joint. "Take another hit first. Something tells me you're gonna need it."

He's right. I'm gonna need it because nothing good can come of Paulina being here. Nothing good will result from Luna's orders being defied.

After passing the weed back to Fender, I make my way toward Luna and the others. When I reach them, Luna glares at me.

"Do you need something?" she huffs.

"Yeah," I say, not backing down or taking her attitude personally. "I need to know why she's here."

"Pivot was just about to tell me." Luna shifts her gaze to Pivot. "Weren't you?"

"It's my fault," Pauline rushes to say and we focus on her. "I, um… I asked her to bring me."

"Looney Tunes, I know you gave me orders," Pivot states with an apologetic tone. "But she was scared. How the hell was I supposed to leave her behind?"

"You left the others behind," Luna counters.

"I did, but…" Pivot turns a saddened look on Pauline.

"The others don't like me," Paulina says and fidgets with her hands. "I was afraid of what would happen to me if I stayed there, especially after all the other vagrants showed up."

I narrow my eyes at her. Vagrants? We're her goddamn lifeline, not trash from the street.

Luna doesn't seem to have the same reaction to the dig but maybe she's too focused on everything else and just didn't pick up on it. Not that it matters. Paulina's scared and that should be a priority.

"Fine," Luna finally says. "Pivot, get her set up in the spare room and she can watch TV while the clubs meet." Luna twists to look at Paulina and reaches out to lift her hands. "I'm sorry you're scared but I need you to trust us, okay?" The girl nods and Luna releases her hands. "Good. Now, we won't be long and when we're done, I'll take you back to the safe house and have a talk with the others."

"Okay."

Pivot walks away with Paulina and Luna releases a pent-up breath.

"Jesus, could this get any more fucked?" she asks me.

"It can always get more fucked." I reach out and rest my hand on her bicep. "Let's just get through this meeting and you'll feel better because we'll have a plan." I lean in and nuzzle her neck. "And if that doesn't help relieve some of your stress, *I will*."

Luna shivers but pulls away quickly and her eyes dart around the room like she's afraid of getting caught doing something wrong. Annoyance flares but I shove it down and convince myself she's just super focused on the problem at hand. And she should be.

Luna walks to the bar and climbs on top of it, stomping her foot on the wood when she straightens. A hushed silence comes over the room and all eyes turn to her.

"First of all, I want to thank the Soulless Kings for stepping up and assisting us. We appreciate it." I want to call bullshit, but I let her continue instead. "We're gonna be getting started in a few minutes, so if you'll all head to our meeting room, that would be great. Feel free to grab a drink first or smoke a little more if you need to. Before you enter the meeting room, please put any weapons and cell phones in the locker outside the door. Also, we don't permit any drugs in the room. You can get it all back when you leave." She takes a deep breath. "Any questions?"

When there are none, Luna hops off the bar and stalks

across the room toward a hallway. I watch in fascination as every DHMC member in the space, other than Pivot, follows. It's clear Luna runs a well-oiled machine and, even if they are a bit defiant at times, they respect her.

"You coming?" Fender calls, pulling me from my trance.

I join my brothers and we all head to the meeting room. The line forming outside the door reminds me of my school days, especially with the locker there. But instead of books and pencils, we're all divesting ourselves of weapons and drugs.

That's where the similarities end. The room itself is dark, yet somehow feminine. Rather than a conference table like we have, there are several couches, set up to form as close to a circle as they can get. Along one wall there are built in bookshelves which are stuffed full.

I stand behind the chair Luna is occupying, and Fender takes a spot next to me. The others line the walls. A piercing whistle brings silence to the room and Luna stands.

"I know we don't all know one another so I'll introduce DHMC members and Fender," she turns to him. "You can introduce SK's."

"Works for me," he agrees.

"I'm Luna, or Looney Tunes, president of Devil's Handmaidens." Luna turns to her right. "This is Mollie, our VP and then there's Spooks, Libs, Stormy, Pivot, Lashes…" She goes on to name the seven other members in the room.

"I'm Fender, president of Soulless Kings. This is Riker, our enforcer." He points to me. "Then we've got Piston, the VP, and Joker, Squirrel, Trainwreck, Greaser, Gibson, Flash…"

After all fifteen of our present members are introduced, Luna takes over.

"As I said out there, we're glad you're here. I'm not real sure where to start so I'll just dive right in." Luna quickly glances at me and then returns her attention to the room at large. "Conrad Templeton… what do we know about him?"

"He's an evil son of a bitch," Trainwreck grits out.

"He is," Luna agrees. "Unfortunately, there are people who don't agree, which makes him and his *organization* dangerous."

"He's deemed himself Lord Luxuria and is the head of The Church of Sinfinite Opportunity," Squirrel says from his spot against the wall.

"The man is fucking untouchable," Mollie states.

"Is he?" Trainwreck asks and the attention shifts to him. "Hear me out. We have a direct link to him, right here in this clubhouse."

"We're not using a child as bait," Luna snaps.

"I'm not suggesting we do," Trainwreck says. "Trust me, I'm well aware of how he and his followers treat children. But we can use her for information, right?"

"We've tried that," Spooks says. "Every single victim that shows up at Jacks and Jills, we grill for info. We get leads but nothing ever pans out because Templeton is always five steps ahead."

"What about Slim?" I ask and then shake my head. "Kenny, I mean. What about him? He said he recognized someone at Jacks and—"

"Javier Bloom," Mollie states. "He finally told me who he recognized and it's Javier."

"Motherfucker!" Luna spits out and glares at me. "You knew that's who he was talking about the night he showed up, didn't you?"

"I figured," I admit. "But you shut down my questions and then we got… sidetracked."

Luna growls, actually fucking growls, at me.

"Ah, who's Javier Bloom?" Fender asks, cutting through the tension between me and Luna.

"He's a member of the club," Mollie says when Luna remains quiet. "He's also a prominent defense attorney."

"Perfect," Trainwreck mutters. "This is why Templeton gets away with everything, how he's able to orchestrate these fucking games and get away with it."

"Games?" Luna asks. "What games?"

"I told you we got sucked into this because of Trainwreck's sister, Trinity," I begin, and she nods. "One of the people we interrogated gave up some information. Basically, Templeton's trafficking ring is centered around these sick games. Abductors, or players, form teams. They're often made up of people with power who can help make sure they don't get caught." I glance at Trainwreck to make sure he's okay as I explain. I know he wants people to believe he is but he's the furthest thing from okay a person can get. "Anyway, every year, there's this tournament. Whoever makes the most money by selling the product wins. It's fucking sick."

"The product being humans." Luna isn't asking… she's figuring it all out.

"Right."

"What the fuck do they win?" Spooks asks.

"That's just it, the guy died before we could get that info."

Luna nods, her face serious, contemplative.

"So, we have Templeton, who runs this cult and uses it to cover up for his human trafficking business. What would it take for people to go along with this? What prize, for lack of a better word, would that many people be drawn to, sell humans to win?"

"Isn't it obvious?" Greaser states. "People will do anything in the name of religion. According to The Church of Sinfinite Opportunity's website, the ultimate goal for each believer is to live in close proximity to Lord Luxuria because he's their ticket to an afterlife called the Land of Sinfinite

Opportunity that's full of everything they've ever dreamed of."

"Jesus," Mollie mutters.

"Not Jesus… Lord fucking Luxuria," Trainwreck snaps.

"I feel like we're missing something," Fender says. "We've got all these pieces, but they don't quite fit." He turns to Luna. "What about Jacks and Jills? How is this all connected to the club?"

"Aside from the fact that we clearly have one of his believers as a member, we funnel victims through there and offer them safe haven. We do everything we can to reconnect them with family or get them set up with a new identity, a new life. Whatever it takes."

"Do you think there are more of the club's members who are connected to Templeton?"

"I'm sure there are," she admits. "We do extensive background checks for each applicant but clearly, we're no match for them."

"What about this Javier Bloom?" I ask. "Does he come in a lot?"

"Every Tuesday and Thursday, like clockwork," Libs says. When curious stares shift her way, she shrugs. "What? He's hot, I've noticed."

"He's also fucking bad news," Luna snaps.

"Yeah, well, I didn't know that until now, did I?"

"Enough!" I shout and Luna shoots daggers at me. "I'm not trying to overstep so don't even start," I tell her. "But fighting amongst all of us can't happen. If we want to have even the smallest of chances of taking down this ring, we need to work together."

Luna heaves a sigh and looks back at Libs. "Sorry, Riker's right. There's strength in numbers but not if we can't function as a solid team."

"Don't worry about it." Libs waves her hand, dismissing Luna's apology. "But I have an idea."

"Spit it out, then."

"Javier has asked me to join him in a private room several times but it's always when I'm working the desk, so I haven't been able to. What if, the next time he comes in, I turn the tables on him?"

"And then what?" Luna asks. "I don't want you in the room alone with him. There's no telling what he'll do, especially if there really is a lead on Paulina's location."

"Wait," I say. "This could work." When Luna opens her mouth to protest, I hold a hand up to stop her. "She won't be alone with him or in any danger. Because you and I will be waiting in the room for him. We can make sure the only available room is the one closest to an exit. We knock his ass out, get him out of Jacks and Jills and take him to the Nightmare Room. We'll interrogate him, get whatever info he has and then use it to take down The Church and Templeton."

"What's the Nightmare Room?"

I grin at Luna.

"Looney Tunes, the Nightmare Room is going to be your new favorite playground."

CHAPTER TWENTY

Ready to get your hands dirty?

Luna

"Do you know how hard it is to stand here and not touch you?"

I swirl the ice in my glass and look at Riker's reflection in the glass of my office. It's been almost a week since our two clubs met and we've both been very busy. I've wanted to spend time with him, see if we could get to a place beyond my safe word but no opportunity has presented itself. There's always someone around.

"There's no time for that," I remind him.

"Trust me, I'm aware." Riker huffs out a breath and starts to pace behind me. "What if he doesn't show up tonight?"

I turn to watch him. His strides are long, determined, angry. He's holding one of his blades, gripping it like a lifeline. One thing I've learned in the last few days is that he does that when he's feeling impatient, ready to strike but no target in sight. It's a huge turn on.

"He'll show up," I assure him. When he doesn't slow down, I step in front of him and flatten a palm on his chest. "It's Thursday. He didn't show up on Tuesday, so he'll be here tonight."

Riker bends and lifts me with his free hand cradling my ass. I wrap my legs around his waist as he backs me into the large window overlooking the main floor of Jacks and Jills.

"I thought you weren't touching me," I tease.

He presses his body against mine to pin me and braces his hands on either side of my head. His knife clanks against the glass and most women would take that as a reminder of how dangerous he is, but not me. Just knowing it's in his hand, knowing it's an extension of him… that's sexy as fuck and makes my pussy clench.

"Not touching you is boring," he whispers before sucking my earlobe into his mouth.

He swirls his tongue and dips to my neck. I throw my head back, completely helpless against his assault. I reach between us and pull his shirt up so I can run my hands over his skin. I dig my nails into his flesh and Riker groans.

He shifts his mouth to mine and slips his tongue between my lips. He tastes like bourbon and sin and the combination is intoxicating. I grind my hips against his, silently demanding more and as he starts to lower his and as he starts to lower his hand to lift my shirt up, a buzzing sound reaches my ears.

"What's that?" I ask after breaking the kiss.

Riker sets me on my feet. "It's my phone."

He reaches into his pocket and pulls it out. He taps on the screen and then lifts his eyes to mine, a grin spreading across his face.

"It's showtime."

Riker flips the phone around for me to see and I read the text from Trainwreck alerting us that Javier has arrived. I push past Riker to check out the security monitors. And there he is, laughing at whatever it is Libs is saying.

And Libs… she's playing the part perfectly. A little too perfectly maybe but I can't worry about that right now. As long as he agrees to go to the private room, that's all that matters. Libs is a big girl and knows what's at stake.

Riker and I head down the back staircase. It doesn't lead to the main room like the other one does and is rarely used, but it serves our purposes now. When we get to the room, we leave the lights turned off and wait.

And we wait and wait and wait some more.

"What is taking so long?" Riker asks when almost an hour passes.

"I don't fucking know," I snap.

I grab my cell and pull up the virtual waiting room app. It shows that Javier booked this room for the entire night, but it doesn't list who his partner is going to be. I close that app and tap on the phone icon to call Libs.

"What the hell is going on?" I bark when she answers.

"He booked the room but—"

"I know he booked the room," I snap. "I checked the app. Why are you not bringing him here?"

"He booked the room but then another member showed up and he got sidetracked with him. They're talking in the corner right now. I tried to interrupt, and it didn't go well. Fucker said to give him another ten minutes."

"Who's he talking to? What member?"

"Manny Collins. He joined a few weeks ago."

"What do we know about him? Is he someone we have to worry about?"

"Nothing popped up in his background check. He's an EMT. His kink is inflicting pain on his partners and then treating them."

"Okay, just… don't take your eyes off of them. And get in here as soon as you can."

"Got it."

Libs ends the call and I fill Riker in on what she said. At the mention of Manny, he seems suspicious but doesn't dwell on it. We both realize that we're going to question pretty much anyone and everyone at this point and we can't do that. At least not outside of DHMC and SKMC members. Doing that could jeopardize us all, not to mention our attempt at taking down Templeton and bringing trouble to the legitimate members of Jacks and Jills.

The electronic lock on the door disengages and it swings open. Javier steps in and Libs pulls the door shut behind him. The man's eyes widen.

"What's the meaning of this?" he asks.

His tone holds an air of authority that he does not appear to feel. His gaze darts around the room and his cheeks turn white as color drains from his face. He turns and twists the doorknob, trying to escape.

"You're Javier Bloom, correct?" Riker asks as he stalks toward him.

"Look, I don't know what you think is going to happen, but I'm not into role playing. That's not my kink."

I laugh but it's hollow. "Oh, we know. Your kink is abduction." I shrug. "Anything for Lord Luxuria, isn't that right?"

"I don't know what you're talking about," Javier counters.

He doesn't visibly react to the mention of Templeton or his games. He's not going to be easy to crack. Giddiness washes over me.

I'm certainly going to have fun trying.

Riker brushes past me and stabs Javier in the neck with a paralytic. I don't know where he got it, but it doesn't matter. Not now anyway. Later, when this is over, I'll ask about his connections. DHMC could use a connection like that.

When Javier starts to fall, Riker scoops him up. "Let's get him out to the van."

We exit the room, careful to make sure there are no members straggling in the hallways to see us carry Javier outside. Riker tosses him into the back of the waiting van and slams the doors shut. He walks around to the driver's window, where Trainwreck is.

"He better be alive when we get there," Riker says, his warning clear.

"He will be," Trainwreck assures him. "He's not the one I want to kill. You two can have him."

Riker smacks the side of the van and Trainwreck pulls out of the lot. When the taillights disappear into the night, Riker turns to me and grins.

"Ready to get your hands dirty?"

I rub my palms together like a greedy kid on Christmas morning.

"So fucking ready."

CHAPTER TWENTY-ONE

Big fucking mistake.

Riker

The ride to Soulless Kings' property is torture. Luna surprised me by agreeing to ride with me and having her on the back of my bike, her body pressed against mine... torture with a side of bliss. My cock could chisel through stone if it had to and I itch to drag her around to the front of me and let her ride me while we, well, ride.

Instead, I'm driving with my hand resting on her thigh, squeezing every few minutes as erotic images flash in my mind, transposing over the road ahead of us. When we reach the property and drive through the gates, I realize the trip was a blur and I have no clue how we arrived in one piece.

I park my bike in front of the clubhouse and let Luna get off first. Before I can stand, she steps in close and reaches between my legs.

"When we're done with Javier…" She palms my crotch and licks her lips. "... I want this."

I don't get a chance to respond because she pulls away and walks toward the porch.

"We're not going in through there," I call out to her. She turns back to me. "Around back."

She follows me around the clubhouse to the entrance that will lead us straight to the Nightmare Room without having to deal with anyone else. When I open the door for her, she hesitates for a second, staring into the dark stairwell with trepidation.

"Can't have fun standing out here," I say and settle my hand on her lower back.

Luna descends the steps and I follow, closing the door behind me. The door to the Nightmare Room is shut but the monitor on the wall is on. Luna's eyes are fixed on the screen, wide and… giddy.

"So," she says, crossing her arms over her chest. "This is the Nightmare Room?"

"Yep."

I punch in the code on the panel next to the door and when it opens, I gesture for Luna to go in first. She steps across the threshold and crosses the room to crouch near Javier's slumped body.

"Looks like Trainwreck had a bit of fun putting him in here," she comments.

I take in the abrasions on Javier's face and chuckle. "Yeah, fucker probably dragged him down the concrete steps. He doesn't have to clean this room anymore, so he doesn't mind adding a little blood here and there."

Luna stands and shifts to face me. "Anymore?"

"When he was a prospect, he was a cleaner more often than not." I shrug. "Now that he's got his patch, he's off the hook and can help make the mess."

"Right."

A groan comes from the corner and we both focus our

attention on our captive. Javier tries to sit up, scooting as close to the wall as he can. His eyes dart toward the door and then settle on us.

"Where am I?"

"My new fun factory," Luna deadpans and cocks her head. "You're not having fun?"

Javier simply looks at her like she's crazy. And I guess, to some, she probably is. To me, she's fucking beautiful, especially in her element.

"Oh, Riker, he's not having fun." Luna elbows me. "How can we change that? I want him to enjoy the last few hours of his life."

"Will you settle for *you* enjoying the last few hours of his life?" I counter. "Because I don't think he's going to like any of it."

"Do you have any idea who I am?" Javier shouts. "You won't get away with this. People will look for me."

"See, that's the thing." Luna crouches again and grips his chin in her hands. She smacks his cheek with the other. "We're counting on it."

In a moment which can only be described as sheer stupidity, or a death wish, Javier shoves against Luna's chest and she falls back on her ass.

I see red. Lots and lots of fucking red.

I bend down and lift him up by his throat until his toes are dangling. Javier scratches at my hands, struggles to get out of my grasp but for an evil fuck, he's weak as hell.

"If you touch her again, I will kill you," I snarl, spit flinging from my lips to his face. "And I really don't want to kill you because I want her to have some fun." I lower him to the floor but don't let go. "Don't make me kill you."

When I drop my hands, he slumps to the floor but quickly scrambles to his feet to scurry to the corner. Pathetic… and very predictable.

I turn to help Luna up and see her already standing, knife in one hand and pistol in the other.

"Well, now, the party's about to start," I say, letting insanity fuel my words and settle in my bones.

"Look, I, um…" Javier stutters. "I'm a really good defense attorney. If you let me go, I'm sure we can work out a deal or something. Maybe I could defend you against any pending charges?"

Bargaining. It always happens in this room. In their desperation, they think they can offer something we give a damn about. And it's usually spurred on by incorrect assumptions about who we are.

"That's the thing," Luna says and closes the distance between them. She pushes the barrel of the gun to his temple. "We're too good to have any charges. I mean, really, do we look that inexperienced at this?"

Fear enters Javier's eyes. It was there already but there's no hiding it any longer. Nothing he can do or say will make that fear disappear now. Because now comes acceptance.

"What do you want from me then?" he asks.

"It's simple," I tell him. "Information. That's all we want. Give us that and we'll think about letting you go."

"Information," he repeats. "All I have to do is answer some questions and I'll walk out of here."

"You'll get out of here, yes," Luna assures him.

Good girl. Don't lie to him if you can help it. And she didn't. Javier Bloom will get out of this room… in a body bag.

Javier's shoulders drop, relief swiftly changing his approach. "Okay then. What do you want to know?"

He looks at me when he asks the question, ignoring the gun still at his temple, the woman holding it.

Big fucking mistake.

Luna pistol-whips him and shouts, "You talk to me, not him!"

Blood trickles from the fresh gash on his head and Javier lifts his hand to put pressure on the wound.

"O-okay," he stutters.

She smacks his cheek again. "Good man."

Luna begins pacing the length of the Nightmare Room, waving the gun around wildly. Her grip on the knife is still tight, like she's simply counting down the seconds until she can strike.

Some would worry that she's unstable, that they would get hurt with the way she's acting. And if I'm being honest, she does seem like a loose cannon. But she's anything but. She's the most stable person who's ever set foot in this room and her actions are deliberate, purposefully misleading.

Luna McAllister is in control and only a danger to anyone who thinks otherwise. Oh, and Javier Bloom. She's definitely a danger to him.

She's a catastrophe waiting to happen with your heart, too.

CHAPTER TWENTY-TWO

It's always interesting to me to witness the moment someone realizes that all their past transgressions have caught up to them.

Luna

Left.
One, two, three, four, five.
Right.
One, two, three, four, five.
Left.

I lose track of how many times I pace the length of the Nightmare Room. Riker is leaning in the corner, arms crossed over his chest, a grin spread across his face. And Javier? Well, he's burning holes through my body with the intensity of his stare, the way he's tracking my every move.

My brain is screaming at me, demanding I shove this blade into his stomach and let him bleed out. And I want to. *Badly*. But then what? Killing Javier doesn't get justice for my mom, it doesn't get revenge or answers.

It will make you feel better.

Maybe for all of ten seconds. And then I'd be back to square one. No, I can't kill him, not yet. But I will.

I pivot for the last time and walk back toward Ja—

"What the fuck?" I mumble as a pungent smell enters my nostrils. I scrunch my nose against it and drop my eyes to the wet crotch of Javier, the puddle under him. "Did you seriously just piss yourself?"

Pointing my pistol at his crotch, I pull the trigger. His scream as he drops to the concrete floor is like music to my ears.

Javier cups his junk and cries like a baby. I throw my head back on a laugh.

"Wh-what's so funny?" he yells.

"Dude," Riker says and comes to stand next to me. "The only thing you're getting on your hands is piss." He kisses me on the cheek. "Nice touch."

I shrug as if it's no big deal when in reality, it's kinda my thing. I like to scare people. I like to play the psychopath—or sociopath… I never can remember the difference—and watch my victim's reaction when I pull the trigger and nothing happens.

And the fact that Riker appreciates it sends shockwaves through my system to settle between my legs.

"You're crazy," Javier accuses.

"Why do you think they call me Looney Tunes?" I counter.

When Javier's eyes widen this time, there's something different in them. The fear is still there but there's also… recognition.

"You're Looney Tunes?"

"I am," I confirm. "And you work for Conrad Templeton."

"Who?"

"Don't," Riker snaps. "Don't pretend you don't know who she's talking about. Conrad Templeton. Lord Luxuria. I don't give a shit if you call him 'daddy' or late for dinner, but don't play stupid."

And there it is, Javier's lightbulb moment. It's always interesting to me to witness the moment someone realizes that all their past transgressions have caught up to them. Interesting and intoxicating and almost as satisfying as submitting to a dom… almost.

"F-fine. What do you want to know about him?"

"Everything!" Luna yells.

"You'll never take him down," Javier says. "He can't be caught. He's made sure of that."

"How?"

"Because he never gets his hands dirty. He's got people for everything."

"He got his hands dirty once, six years ago," I snap. "When he killed my mother."

"Oh my God," Javier mumbles, more of that recognition bleeding into his expression. "That's why he wants to take you out."

"Excuse me?"

"Why do you think I'm a member at Jacks and Jills? It's certainly not the atmosphere, although I don't mind a good fucking every once in a while, when my other *purchases* don't get the job done."

The way he says 'purchases', talks about flesh and blood people like they're a loaf of bread he buys off the grocery store shelf pokes at my already fractured soul. Javier's brand of evil isn't anything new to me, but the visceral reaction is always the same, no matter how used to it I think I am.

"My Lord has spent millions trying to infiltrate Jacks and Jills. To hear him tell it, the day he killed your mom, he knows how close he came to getting caught." Javier shakes his head as if we're children and need him to dumb it down for us. "There was a deviant there, in the building. He wanted to make it look like an accident, a scene gone wrong. But he heard someone else in the building. Somehow, she got out of the room and when he realized they were actually alone, he shot her."

Tears burn the back of my eyes and threaten to spill over. I take a deep breath, then another, and another. I have to maintain control for as long as possible if I want to get more answers. But hearing the callous way he describes the day my mom was murdered is almost too much. And knowing that, if not for the measures she took and I continue to take to ensure privacy, Riker may have heard something and been able to save her.

"Why?" I ask, already suspecting the answer but needing to know for sure.

"Why did he kill her?" Javier asks for clarification.

I nod.

He shrugs. "She said 'no'."

I drop to my knees and plunge the knife I'm holding into his thigh. He howls in pain, and I twist the blade.

"To what?" I demand, putting all of my weight on the handle to inflict the maximum amount of pain.

Javier mutters incoherently. He tries to grab a hold of me, any part of me he can, in an effort to get me to stop. He kicks his uninjured leg and thrashes his arms, but I don't budge. I won't budge. I can't budge. He deserves everything I'm doing to him and more.

"What did she say 'no' to?" I ask again.

"Using Jacks and Jills as a front for his operation," he finally spits out.

I remove the knife from his leg and stand, wiping the blood off on my jeans as I do. I start to pace the room, needing an outlet for all the emotions threatening to burst from me from the inside out.

"Why did he put you in the club?" Riker asks. "What's his plan?"

As I wait for Javier's answer, I listen to the erratic thumping of my heartbeat in my ears, try to match the thud of my footsteps to it. Something about the meaningless task calms me.

"He put me there for several reasons," Javier admits.

"What reasons?"

"He recently lost his most profitable team and he wanted me to find a replacement."

I stop pacing and tower over Javier. "That's only one reason. What are the others?"

"He still wants Jacks and Jills to be used to his advantage. Funnel product through, recruit more teams… he'll do anything to make that happen."

"Did you find a replacement?"

Javier averts his gaze for a moment and then returns it to me. "Not yet."

His tone is filled with disappointment and regret. If he's to be believed, he failed at his mission. I can only imagine what that means for him in The Church of Sinfinite Opportunity. Fortunately for him, he'll never have to face his punishment because he's not going to make it out of this room alive. So really, I'm doing him a favor.

"Are you the only soldier with boots on the ground at Jacks and Jills?" Riker asks.

Javier says nothing but the twitch of his eye gives him away. *No, he's not.*

"Who else is there?" I demand, bending down in front of him again. When he says nothing, I press the gun to his chin. "Who else?"

"There's no one," he cries.

"Forgive me for not believing you."

"It doesn't matter if you believe me."

"That's where you're wrong," I snarl. "It does matter because your life depends on what I get from you, on what I believe."

"You don't get it, do you?" Javier says, his face relaxing.

"Get what?" Riker asks as he crouches down next to me.

"Lord Luxuria will stop at nothing to get what he wants. And his loyal followers will do the same."

"And he wants Jacks and Jills and my head on a stick?" I ask, summing up what I know.

"He wants the world." Javier shrugs. "He wants to play God. He wants every last human on the planet to join The Church of Sinfinite Opportunity and do his bidding."

"Jesus," Riker mutters.

"Ask him about his daughter."

I startle at the sound of the voice coming through what can only be an intercom system. I recognize it as Trainwreck's. I push down my anger at being interrupted and stand to look at Riker. He's got his cell phone in his hand and is tapping the screen. After a second, he starts talking.

"How long have you been watching, Trainwreck?" he asks.

"Long enough."

I turn in a circle, searching the corners for cameras, speakers, anything to piece together how this room actually works. I find what I'm looking for, but they blend in well with the concrete walls and I can see how easy they would be to miss, especially if you're being tortured.

"What else can this room do?" I ask Riker, awe in my tone.

"Pretty much anything we want it to. If it doesn't do it already, we can make it happen if given a few days to make the adjustments."

He shrugs like it's nothing. And maybe to him, it is,

because it's routine. But to me, it's Christmas morning and I've just opened the most coveted toy of the season.

"Here, check this out."

Riker taps his screen again and two chains, with handcuffs on the ends, drop from the ceiling. I tip my head back and see the opening they're suspended from. I didn't even hear it move.

"When this is all over, I'm gonna need you to build me one of these at DHMC clubhouse."

"I think I can make that happen," Riker says and steps toward me. He cups my cheeks and rubs his thumbs under my eyes. "I told you this would be fun."

His lips crash into mine and I lose myself in the warmth his body provides, in the kiss. Riker had already started to burn down the walls I erected to protect myself but now? They're ash. I knew the moment I first saw him, years ago, that he was different.

"Get a fucking room," Trainwreck grits out.

Riker and I break apart, both of us grinning. He rubs his finger over my bottom lip, and I suck it into my mouth, swirling my tongue around it.

"Soon," he growls. "Real fucking soon."

"It's only going to be soon if you take care of that prick in there."

Trainwreck's tone is full of anger, clipped. I take a deep breath and turn back to face Javier, who's now standing with his back pressed against the wall, trying to walk toward the door. Stupid man thinks he can escape? Not likely. I could fuck Riker and kill Javier at the same time and end up satisfied on two fronts.

"Wanna string him up?" Riker asks, stepping next to me and crossing his arms. His tone is relaxed, matter of fact. "Could be fun."

Javier starts to plead with us not to do that, but Riker drags him away from the wall and cuffs him to the chains. They're low enough that he can stand flat-footed and that needs to change.

"Can you raise him up a bit?" I ask Riker.

"Of course," he scoffs.

He does something with his phone again and Javier is lifted off the floor, dangling like a rag doll from the ceiling. He strains to touch his toes to the concrete but there's several inches between the two.

An idea hits me, and I grin at Riker. "Got any more chains?"

Within seconds, two more descend from the ceiling, falling closer to the opposite wall. I look from Javier's hands to the new set of chains and then at Javier's face. He's crying, sobbing really, but he's no longer begging for his life. I drop my eyes to his junk and see that he's hard.

Sick fuck.

"Even now, when you're bleeding and scared, you can't stop your reaction to this, can you?" I ask. I grab his legs and attach them to the new set of chains, talking as I do. "I remember that now, that you always wanted one of the bondage rooms. Being tied up gets you off. Pain, receiving and inflicting it, gets you off." When he's strung up like a hammock, I go to his head and tap his nose with my knife blade. "Well buckle up buttercup, this is gonna be the wildest ride of your life."

Javier whimpers and if I'm not mistaken, there's no fear in it, only desperate need. I take my knife and cut all of his clothes off, making sure to slice his skin in a few places. When he's naked, I return to stand at his head.

"Look at me," I demand.

He twists his head to the side and locks eyes with me.

"Mr. Bloom," I say. "Would you please tell the court your sexual orientation?"

"Wh-what?"

I lean close, close enough to see his pupils dilate, smell the excitement oozing from his pores. "In case you haven't figured it out, we're role playing. You're some big shot attorney, right?" He nods frantically. "Good, your role should be easy. And me… I'm playing judge, jury, and executioner." I step back. "I'll ask you again counselor, what is your sexual orientation?"

"I, uh…" He licks his lips. "Both. I like both."

"Both what?" I demand and shove the tip of the blade into his armpit. "Men, women, sheep… what?!"

"G-girls. Girls and boys."

I yank the knife out and step toward his hips before dropping down to crouch under his suspended body. Blood drips from him to the floor, leaving traces of him in the concrete.

"The daughter," Trainwreck begs through the intercom again. "What do you know about Templeton's daughter?"

"Trainwreck, leave," Riker seethes. "Turn the monitor off and get the fuck out of the hall."

"I'm not—"

"Now!"

The speakers crackle and I know they've been turned off. I don't mind having an audience, but I appreciate Riker stepping in and giving me the space to do this my way, without interference from his own.

"He's gone," Riker tells me. "Please, continue. This is the best show I've been to in a long fucking time."

"Thanks," I say with a grin. "I think I will." I return my attention back to Javier and toss the knife to the floor. "Trainwreck is right, though. I need to know what Templeton knows about his daughter's disappearance."

Javier doesn't respond and I glance up to see his head lolled to the side, his eyes closed. I smack his ass to wake him up and he comes to in a panic.

"Wh-what?"

"What does Templeton know about where his daughter is?" I ask again.

"Nothing," he babbles. "He doesn't know anything."

I shove the barrel of my gun between his cheeks and push up, past his tight hole. Javier's babbling becomes desperate as he tries to buck his hips to get away from the intrusion.

"Don't pretend you don't like this," I say and manipulate the gun, back and forth, in and out. "And don't forget that your life depends on your answers." Javier says nothing. "Fine, you leave me no—"

"Everything!" Javier shouts. "He knows everything."

"Everything?"

"Yes," he confirms.

"Where did he get his information?" I demand, pushing the gun as far as it'll go.

"Where he gets all of his information."

"And where's that?" Riker asks with a bite to his tone.

"From a source."

"No shit," I snarl. "Who is the source?"

"I don't know."

"Bullshit!"

"I swear, I d—"

I squeeze the trigger. Blood splatters across my face and I try to wipe it off with the back of my hand. I stand and turn to Riker, who's brows are raised and eyes are wide.

"Finish him."

CHAPTER TWENTY-THREE

I don't know exactly how or when that happened but I'm pretty sure it was somewhere between her submitting to me when I was trying to earn her trust and shoving a gun up a guy's ass and pulling the trigger, showing me she trusts me completely.

Riker

Finish him.

When I brought Luna to the Nightmare Room, I knew she'd like it, but I don't think anything could have prepared me for just how much. When I use this room, when I torture and kill people in here, I walk away from it confident in the fact that I do what I have to do, that the people deserve what I do to them.

Watching her pull that trigger, seeing the satisfaction she gets from things normal people would find horrific... it's like looking into a mirror of my soul. My black, disturbed soul. And I love it. I love—

"Finish him."

I shake my head to clear my vision and see Luna standing near the door. I shift my eyes to the man she strung up. He's not conscious and I'm pretty sure already dead but reach around to grab my gun out of my waistband and point it at his head. I pull the trigger and his head whips to the other side. If he wasn't, he is now.

"Thank you," Luna says.

I lock eyes with her. "For what?"

"For letting me do this." She tips her head toward Javier. "For not freaking out and letting me handle it the way I needed to."

I walk around the hanging body, needing to be close to her. I reach out and wipe a splotch of blood off her forehead.

"You're welcome."

"We need to figure out who Templeton's source is." Luna squares her shoulders. "If he knows where Paulina is, we're screwed. He can't find her. He can't find the safe houses. We promised to protect everyone in them and if he comes for his daughter, he'll find them. I can't let tha—"

"Stop."

Luna narrows her eyes at me. "What?"

"We'll do all of that." I thread my fingers through the hair at the base of her neck. "I promise. But first, you should get a shower and have a drink or two."

"I can shower and drink later," she snaps. "There's too much to do."

"And I need you to trust me when I tell you that you need to take a breath and process what just happened. You can call Mollie and the others and make sure they're alert and ready for anything. Fender will send some Soulless Kings to help." I lean next to her ear. "But right now, I need you to let me take care of you. Because whether you realize it or not, you're running on adrenaline and that's going to disappear soon, and you'll crash. You won't want to, you'll fight it, but you won't be able to stop it."

"And him?" she asks. "What do we do about him?"

"I'll get Royal to clean this up, take him out of here and bury him somewhere." I press a quick kiss to her lips. "It's better if you don't know where."

Luna takes several deep breaths and nods. "Okay."

We spend the next few minutes making necessary phone calls and ensuring that all of the safe houses are secure, and that Javier's body will be taken care of. Mollie begs Luna to come home but Luna stands her ground and assures her VP that she'll be fine with me. When I hear her say that my heart skips a beat and I hold on to the feeling.

When we exit the Nightmare Room, Royal is already in the hall, waiting with a grin on his face. His eyes land on Luna and he grins.

"Damn. Must've been a good night."

"You have no idea," Luna says.

"But you're about to," I tell him and hitch a thumb over my shoulder. "I hope you've got an empty stomach because that's, well… the result of a good night."

"Got it."

"I don't want to see your face until the body is disposed of," I add.

"Yep, got it, Riker."

"Good."

I lead Luna past him and up the steps. When we step out into the fresh air, she pauses and lets her head fall back. She takes several deep breaths, as if doing so cleanses her. I watch, focusing on the column of her throat and then letting my gaze travel lower, over her chest, down her body.

Emotion slams into me, threatening to knock me off my feet. Luna is like no other woman I've ever met. She's beautiful, feisty, and exactly who I need in my life. I recognize that I haven't known her long. Shit, I still don't know her well. But I know enough.

Luna is perfectly imperfect and just the right amount of 'looney' to be perfect for me.

"Riker?"

I lift my gaze back to her face, trying to ignore the fact that my heart is threatening to pound out of my chest, trying like hell to not let her see the thoughts running through my head. It's not easy because I want to blurt it all out, tell her I love her and would do anything to show her.

Holy shit. I love her.

I don't know exactly how or when that happened but I'm pretty sure it was somewhere between her submitting to me when I was trying to earn her trust and shoving a gun up a guy's ass and pulling the trigger, showing me she trusts me completely. Because who does that in front of someone they don't trust?

"Riker, are you okay?" she asks when I stand there like an idiot, silent and contemplative.

"Never better."

"Then take me to the nearest shower and a bed."

I grab her hand and tug her around the clubhouse to my Harley. She settles behind me and I drive us to my cabin. When I park, I sit there for a few minutes, soaking up the way her arms are wrapped around me and her head is resting against my back. It feels good, right.

We finally get off the bike and I lift her in my arms to carry her inside. I set her down in the bathroom and methodically take her clothes off. As I peel the bloody garments from her body, she doesn't move. I reach around her to turn the water on and once it's hot, I guide her under the spray.

"Are you coming in?" she asks sleepily, the adrenaline wearing off.

"Do you want me to?"

She nods and covers a yawn with her hand.

I strip my clothes off and toss them into the corner with hers. I step over the ledge, and she shifts to give me room behind her. I wrap my arms around her stomach and pull her back toward me.

We stand like that, her pressed tightly against me, water running over our heads to swirl in a crimson tide down the drain. There's nothing sexual about it but my dick doesn't get the memo.

"Riker, I don't think I—"

"Shhh." I kiss her neck. "It's fine, Luna," I whisper in her ear. "I can't help the way I react to you but I'm a grown ass man and know when the time is all wrong."

"I'm sorry," she mumbles and yawns again.

I straighten and slowly spin her around before tilting her face up so I can look her in the eyes.

"I'm only going to tell you this once so listen up." She lowers her eyes and my cock twitches. Damn her submissive tendencies. "You don't ever have to say you're sorry when it comes to sex. Not when you're not in the mood, not when you say your safe word. Never. And I won't ever apologize for how much I want you because that's out of my control. Okay?"

"Okay."

"Good. Now let me take care of you."

I spend the next ten minutes washing blood from Luna's hair and skin, massaging the tension from her body. When I'm done with her, I concentrate on myself and then turn the water off. I dry us both off and carry her to my bedroom, where I lay her on the mattress and pull the blanket over her.

"Where are you going?" she asks when I don't join her.

"I'm just gonna grab my phone out of the bathroom. I'll be right back."

I'm gone for less than thirty seconds but she's asleep when I return. Good. She needs the rest.

I crawl in beside her and she flips over to curl into my side. Luna throws a leg over mine and sighs as her body relaxes in sleep.

I stare at the ceiling for a long time, replaying the last few weeks in my head. It's been a roller coaster and at first, I wanted off. But now, it's my favorite ride and I'll happily stay on it for the rest of my life.

My eyes begin to droop, and I press a kiss to Luna's head, letting my lips linger for a long moment.

"Love you."

CHAPTER TWENTY-FOUR

This, my love, is true. It's scary and fast and wonderful and very true.

Luna

Love.

I've felt it before. But this, this feeling of falling off a cliff with nothing but hope and a prayer that someone will catch you before you hit the ground? This is new.

I focus on Riker's heartbeat against my palm, the way his breathing remains even, the peaceful look on his face as he sleeps.

A memory of a long-ago conversation with my mom surfaces.

"Mom, how do you know when you're in love?"

My mom sets the clean beer mug on the bar top and smiles at me. "You just do."

"But how?" I demand, frustrated. "I mean, I've watched movies and stuff, but it can't really be like that, can it?"

"Like what?"

"Fast. Seriously, who falls in love with someone they just met? It's crazy. And it's stupid."

Mom leans her elbows on the bar. "Why is it crazy?"

"Because," I whine. "Like, in a movie, it's fake. You can't meet someone and then a few days later love them. And you definitely can't fall in love with someone you hate. That can't really be how it works."

"My love, why the sudden interest in how love works?"

I hop off my stool in a huff of frustration. "I don't know."

"Who is he?"

I heave a sigh and roll my eyes. I shouldn't have said anything because now she won't stop until I tell her what she wants to know. I give in. "Only the cutest boy in school. And I used to hate him but today..." I can't stop the stupid smile on my face. "He was nice to me today and I think I might love him."

"Oh, Luna," Mom chastises with a cluck of her tongue. "You're only twelve years old. Of course you think you love him."

"What's that supposed to mean?" I demand, only becoming more confused every time she opens her mouth.

"Luna, my love, when you love someone, really love them, you'll know." She walks around the bar to wrap an arm around my shoulders and pull me close. "Love is like... well, it's like jumping off a cliff. Sometimes people jump because they're sad and trying to find peace or cling to something good. Other people jump because they feel like they have to or because they think it's what they're supposed to do." She taps my nose. "That's not true love. Those people, they only think they're in love, that jumping is the answer to all their problems. Low self-esteem? Love will fix it. Depression? Love will fix it. Getting older or have a ticking biological clock? Love will fix it."

"But what about true love?"

"True love is different, special," she says. "When it's true love, it still feels like jumping off a cliff. But you're not jumping because you have to. You're jumping because you can't help it. You're *jumping because it doesn't matter what is waiting for you at the end of the fall. You're jumping because the thought of not jumping, of not taking the risk, is unbearable. You're jumping because, whether or not you realize it, you're hoping the person you love is jumping with you and you'll both grow wings and fly away together."*

"That makes no sense."

"True love doesn't always make sense. It doesn't have to. It just... is."

Love.

I feel it with Riker. It's unexplainable, unpredictable, and not at all what I was expecting to feel in such a short time. But it just… is.

"Are you going to stare at me all morning?"

I sigh and smile at Riker. "How long have you been awake?"

"Long enough to hear you say 'it just is', whatever that means."

I throw the covers off of us and sit up, groaning in frustration that apparently some of my thoughts were leaking from my lips.

"Is that all you heard?" I ask.

Riker narrows his eyes at me. "Yeah, why?"

"No reason."

He sits up quickly and rolls me over so he's straddling me. "You sure about that?"

"If I'm not, what are you gonna do about it?" I taunt.

Riker pretends to think for a moment, staring past me at the headboard. When his eyes return to mine, his face is hard, his jaw set.

"Remember your safe word?" he demands.

A flutter of excitement rushes between my thighs. "Of course."

"Good." He moves off of me and stands next to the bed. "Use it if you need to."

Before I know what he's doing, he grabs my arms and pulls me to stand with him. He flips our positions and sits on the edge of the mattress.

"On your knees," he commands.

I drop to the floor and rest my palms on his thighs.

"Did I say you could touch me?"

I yank my hands back and fold them in front of me. "No, sir."

"That's right," he confirms. "Put my cock in your mouth."

I lean forward, hands still clasped in front of me, and touch my lips to his mushroomed tip. I dart my tongue out, swirl it around his head before sucking his length into my mouth until it touches the back of my throat.

"Holy shit," Riker mutters as his fingers thread in my hair.

I hum with him still in my mouth, knowing the vibrations will spur him on. As I suck him off, my pussy throbs. With seemingly no control over my movement, my hands shift to my clit, and I rub it.

"It's okay," he groans. "Touch yourself all you want. But if you come before I give you permission, there will be consequences."

I work my tongue around him, swallowing when he's at his deepest, all the while rubbing circles over my clit and trying to pay attention, so I don't explode.

"Fucking hell," he growls. "I'm gonna come, Luna. I'm gonna fucking paint your mouth and you're gonna take it like the good girl you are."

Two seconds later, Riker does exactly what he said he would, and I swallow every last drop. What I don't do is stop playing with my clit.

Riker lifts me to my feet and yanks my hand away. I moan at the loss of pressure, but I know he'll take care of me. He guides me backward until I run into the wall on the other side of the room and his mouth crashes into mine.

My hands are everywhere: his face, his chest, his hips. Any inch of skin I can touch, I do. I moan into his mouth, giving my pleasure to him, begging him to give it back, give me more.

"What do you want, Luna?" he demands.

"You, Riker," I breathe. "I want you."

He drops his hand and shoves a finger into my pussy, then adds a second. "Do you need me, Luna? Need this?"

"Yes."

He thrusts his fingers in, out, in out. He's rough and brutal and it only serves to make me the wettest I've ever been.

Riker drops to his knees and as he continues to finger fuck me, he flattens his tongue to my clit and drags it up, down, up, down. I come unglued.

"Ahhh," I shout into the room.

"That's it," he growls against me. "Ride it out."

Riker doesn't slow down until my legs stop trembling and my knees buckle. He catches me before I hit the floor and eases me down onto my back.

"That was just the beginning," he whispers before pressing a quick kiss to my lips. "Now, I'm gonna fuck you until you're begging me to stop."

I grin and nod. "Okay."

Riker positions himself on top of me and pushes just the tip in. Unable to wait, I grab his hips and pull him forward. His cock is thrust into me as far as it'll go, and I see heaven.

I lift my hips, seeking as much contact with him as I can get. He lowers his head and sucks a nipple into his mouth, gently sinking his teeth into the bud and soothing it with his tongue.

We fuck like two people who need it to survive. It's fast

and frenzied and when my pussy clamps down around him, his dick throbs. He continues to slam into me as my orgasm tears through my body. We're both shouting out our releases, as if that's the only way to make sure they don't rip us apart from the inside out.

When Riker collapses on top of me, I savor the weight of him. His sweat mingles with mine, his heartbeat thumps wildly, in sync with mine. In this moment, we're one. We're the same.

And I'm hopelessly in love with him.

Riker rolls to the side, taking me with him and tucking me into his side. Three words sit on the tip of my tongue, like a kid sitting on a diving board and trying to convince himself to jump off for the first time.

This, my love, is true. It's scary and fast and wonderful and very true.

My mom's voice haunts me, and at the same time, it gives me the push I need.

"Riker?"

"Hmm?"

"I…" I take a deep breath and lift myself up on my arm so I can look at him. "I'm…"

"I love you too, Luna."

CHAPTER TWENTY-FIVE

If you hurt me or break my heart... Soulless Kings MC will be my next villain.

Riker

"This is a bit fast, don't ya think?"

For the last week, I've been answering the same question, defending my feelings for Luna when they aren't defendable. I agree with everyone, it's fast, but it feels right and I'm choosing to focus on that.

"Greaser, if someone asked you that about Trinity, what would you say?"

"Low blow, dude," he snaps.

I tip my beer bottle to my lips and swallow the last of its contents. After tossing the empty into the trash, I clap Greaser on the back.

"Brother, it wasn't meant that way," I tell him. "All I'm saying is I don't think there is such a thing as fast when it comes to matters of the heart."

"Fuck, now you're starting to sound like a douche," he accuses and rolls his eyes. "It's pathetic."

"Leave him alone," Squirrel says when he joins us. "Love isn't this one size fits all thing."

"Oh my God," Gibson whines when he settles next to me. "You've all gone soft."

"I haven't gone soft," Squirrel objects. "I'm just telling it like it is."

"And what do you know about love?" Greaser asks him. "I've never seen you with the same bitch twice."

Squirrel averts his eyes but not before something flashes in them. Pain, heartache? Who knows? Squirrel isn't an open book when it comes to personal shit. He's as loyal a brother as any but he's always kept a part of him separate, distant.

"Did you find anything?" I ask him in an attempt to put him out of his misery.

"No," Squirrel admits and his face morphs into a mask of frustration. "No phone calls that stand out, nothing that would indicate that Templeton knows where Paulina is." He shrugs. "Sorry, brother. I know you and Luna were hoping Javier was telling the truth and that this would end quickly but I don't think that's gonna happen."

"It's okay," I tell him. "Stay on it though. I don't want anything or anyone to slip past us or DHMC. Luna's constantly on edge and I have a feeling she will be until this is over."

"At least she has you to make it all better," Greaser teases.

"You of all people should know there are some wounds nothing can heal," I remind him. "I can protect her, I can make her feel good, I can love her. What I can't do is take away her need for revenge or dim the part of her that craves taking on all the evil in the world. Nor do I want to."

"What are you fuckers standing around bitching about?"

I whirl around and see Fender striding toward us, a beer in one hand and a joint in the other.

"Oh, you know," I say. "Vaginas and evil."

"So Luna and Templeton?" he counters.

"Something like that."

"I take it the deep dive into phone records didn't give us anything," Fender says to Squirrel.

"Unfortunately, no."

"I didn't think we would," Fender states. "He's too good. And he has way more people to protect him than we're used to."

"Don't tell Luna I said this, but I wasn't exactly hopeful either," I admit.

"Your secret's safe with me." Fender puffs on the joint and passes it to me. "But you should be honest with her. If this is going to work between the two of you, there can't be secrets."

"Do you tell Charlie everything?" I counter.

"That's not a fair question. You know I don't tell her about club business. But Luna's different. She's the fucking president of her own MC. And if we're going to keep working with them, our business is her business."

"That's not going to be an easy habit to break, the secrecy."

"Of course it's not. But it'll be worth it."

I let Fender's words sink in. He's right. I can't keep anything from Luna. Even when, to me, it's the most basic, trivial thing. She's not like the other ol' ladies. Charlie grew up in an MC, so she knows the score, and the women? They came into their relationships being told up front how it worked.

"I'll talk to her tonight, at the party."

"Yes, the party," Squirrel says. "Any idea what to expect?"

"It's a party, man," Greaser quips. "Booze and babes."

"It's a party at an all-female MC clubhouse. Two sets of bikers and lots of alcohol, hopefully some skunky lettuce." Squirrel chuckles. "Nothing about this is going to be a normal party."

"But damn it'll be fun."

The line of bikes parked in front of the DHMC clubhouse is impressive. With everything going on, I didn't expect there to be this many people. I pull around to the side of the building and park. My brothers follow my lead and when all the engines are cut, we descend upon the clubhouse.

"Oh shit," Squirrel says and nods toward a group of ladies in the corner. They remind me of our Bangin' Betty's, barely there clothes and sex appeal for days. Do female clubs have club whores? "If you need me, you know where to find me."

"Between some bitches legs?" Trainwreck laughs.

"Exactly," Squirrel confirms and walks away from us.

I shake my head at him even as I search the room for Luna. I spot Mollie and Spooks at the bar, talking with a few other women I don't recognize. Libs and Pivot are behind the bar, serving drinks and flirting with anything with a pulse, male or female.

"If your girlfriend caught you staring like that, she might get jealous."

I whirl around and my breath catches in my throat. Luna is wearing a pair of tight jeans, black biker boots, and a red tank top that barely comes high enough to cover her nipples. Add in her cut and sinful grin and my own jeans no longer fit.

I swallow the saliva that's pooled under my tongue and reach out to haul her to me. Lifting her face, I settle my lips against hers. She matches my passion, sweeping her tongue into my mouth, swirling it around mine.

"And I would remind her that she has absolutely nothing to worry about," I growl when she breaks the kiss. "Absolutely nothing."

"Good to know."

"So…"

I rock back on my heels, not sure what to talk about. I'm used to seeing her at Jacks and Jills or in full badass bitch mode. Relaxed at a party, letting loose and having fun is a side of her that's new to me.

"Don't do that," she snaps.

"What?"

"Make it weird," she clarifies. "We've done the whole 'I love you' thing, we've fucked, we've even slept together. It's a relationship, Riker. Not a firing squad."

I laugh nervously. "I know it's a relationship. But…"

"What?"

"I know this will come as a shock, but I don't do relationships."

"Not exactly breaking news." Luna slips her arm through mine. "And neither do I." She shakes her head. "Correction… neither *did* I. But here we are."

"Here we are," I repeat.

What the fuck is wrong with me? Why am I all of a sudden acting like a teenage boy with acne and no self-confidence?

Because it's Luna. You love her and you're terrified you're gonna fuck it up.

"Come with me."

Luna drags me across the room and out a side door. The smell of weed assails my nostrils and I inhale, silently begging to get a contact high. It doesn't work but it was a nice thought.

"Hey, Looney Tunes!"

Luna stops, forcing me to do the same, and turns to the left. It's dark out but the flood lights on the corners of the roof illuminate a group of people. Some are wearing DHMC cuts and others are sporting Soulless Kings cuts. A blunt is being passed around as smoke billows in the air.

"Where are you going?" the same voice asks.

"I'm gonna go fuck this guy, Lashes," Luna shouts back. "Got a problem with it?"

"No, ma'am," Lashes responds.

I look over my shoulder and see the woods lining the property. There's a clear entrance to what appears to be a path.

"You're dragging me in the woods for sex?" I ask, completely okay with that plan.

"No, but she doesn't need to know that."

Luna resumes tugging me to the woods, and I let go of the disappointment of knowing I'm not gonna get laid in the next few minutes.

"What *are* we doing then?"

"You'll see."

Luna sounds so happy I don't have the heart to push. The further into the woods we get, the more relaxed she becomes. After several minutes, we reach a clearing and the trees seem to disappear, or at least become less dense. Motion lights activate, illuminating the space.

Luna drops my hand and walks across the clearing. I watch as she pulls slabs of wood out of a large truck and sets them up. They look like targets when she's done but targets for what, I have no idea.

"Have a seat," she instructs and points to my right.

That's when I see the bench. It's small and concrete and doesn't look the least bit comfortable.

"Riker, c'mon," she prods. "Trust me."

Whether she knows it or not, I do trust her. So I sit. And the cold seeps through my jeans and chills my ass. I was right, it's not comfortable.

Luna comes toward me but rather than sitting down, she

bends to open small crates that are positioned next to the bench. When she pulls out two axes, I grin.

"Seriously? Ax throwing?"

"It always calms me down." She shrugs. "We've both had a long week, constantly on edge, and I figured this would let us blow off steam. You have the Nightmare Room and I have this."

I stand and wrap my arms around her waist. "I love it."

"Of course you do." Her tone is clipped, matter of fact.

I don't know how many axes we throw or who's better at it but in what feels like less time than it takes to blink, the sun is peeking through the trees. We spent the night talking about everything and nothing. I now know her favorite color is black because it disguises blood, and her favorite ice cream flavor is vanilla because she can add whatever she wants to it depending on her mood. And she knows I hate the beach but love the smell of the ocean.

What she doesn't know is what Squirrel found, or didn't find, and that needs to change.

"I need to tell you something," I say as I hand her the last ax to put away.

"No, Riker, you don't."

"Yeah, Luna." I grab her hand and force her to stop moving and look at me. "I don't want to keep secrets from you."

"Are you married?"

"What? No."

"Do you have kids somewhere?"

"Of course not."

"Are you a serial killer?"

"Depends on who you ask," I answer honestly. "I'm not the type of killer you see on Dateline, but I do kill without an ounce of guilt."

"Me too," she says and taps a finger to her chin like she's

seriously thinking about all the things she would have a problem with. "I know… you fucked my mom."

"Jesus." I take a step back. "No. She was my mentor and friend, nothing else."

"Then there's nothing you need to tell me."

"Would you be serious?" I plead. "This is impo—"

"Squirrel didn't find anything." She turns away from me and bends to mess with the axes in the box. "It's fine. I didn't think he would."

"You knew that's what I was going to tell you, didn't you?

Luna takes a deep breath and sits in the dirt. "Riker, I'm the president of one-percenters. Not only does that make me keenly aware of the kinds of secrets bikers keep, but it also means I can read people pretty well."

I sit down next to her. "I'm sorry. I know you were counting on information." I rest my hand on her knee. "We'll find something, I promise."

"Don't make promises you can't keep."

"I'm not," I assure her. "You know what's at stake for me and my family. You know why we're in this. Add in that Templeton hurt you and I will spend every single day that I draw breath keeping that promise."

"I just want it to be over, ya know?" She lifts her eyes to mine. "Don't get me wrong, my club will always be a safe haven for victims, and we'll always fight against evil. I just want to be up against someone other than Templeton. Someone who didn't ruin my life and the lives of so many others."

"Taking him out won't stop anything." When she glares at me, I add, "Okay, maybe it'll stop The Church of Sinfinite Opportunity, but there are always going to be people like him, people who get their jollies off at the expense of others."

"I know."

I take a deep breath. "Can I ask you something?"

"Sure."

"What comes next?"

"What do you mean?"

"When you defeat Templeton and his minions, what's next? Who's the next villain?"

"I don't know. I've been fighting him for so long I've never thought about it."

"Do you think a partnership with the Soulless Kings is something you'd want to continue, after Templeton?"

"As long as you're in my life, yes. But if you hurt me or break my heart…"

"What?"

"Soulless Kings MC will be my next villain."

CHAPTER TWENTY-SIX

The world didn't end because I took a nap.

Luna
Three weeks later...

"I'm so excited to be here. I've been wanting to come for…"

I tune out the man's words and stare at the counter. I've been working the desk at Jacks and Jills, stepping out of the comfort of my office and onto the front lines because I can't quit waiting for the other shoe to drop.

"Uh, ma'am?"

I lift my eyes to the potential new member. It's Free for All day and based on the fact that he's the forty-second person I've signed in tonight, it's one of our most successful. Riker begged me to cancel it, but I refused. I can't change how I run my business because there's a threat. If I did that, I might as well close Jacks and Jills and crawl in a hole. No, this is my legacy.

"I'm sorry, what were you saying?" I ask him, praying like

hell he doesn't repeat every single word.

"Just that I was done with the paperwork."

He slides the clipboard across the counter, and I snatch it up. I scan his information, transferring the relevant details to my iPad: name, occupation, experience. The rest will be entered later, once we close for the night.

I grab a blue wristband and hand it to him.

"Keep this on at all times," I instruct. "It identifies you as a potential member and someone who is relatively new to BDSM. Regular members will be wearing a red one."

He secures it on his arm and shakes it out, as if testing whether or not it will stay on. "Anything else I need to know?" he asks, letting his gaze drop to my chest.

"That if you keep eye-fucking her, I'll kill you."

I glance over my shoulder to see Riker stepping through the secondary door to the club.

"I'm sorry," Jack—according to his paperwork—mumbles. "I wasn't trying to be disrespectful."

"Pay attention to wristbands and you'll be fine, Jack," I tell him.

Riker puts his arm around me possessively and seethes. While he has nothing to worry about, I kind of like it. Maybe not in front of my customers but other than that, it's not so bad having someone want to protect me for a change.

"Right," Jack says, nodding. "Blue for newbies and red for regulars."

"And then there's green," Riker states. "If two people seem to already be partnered up and neither, or only one of them, is wearing a green band, walk away. They don't want to deal with you. But if they both have green, it means they're open to threesomes."

"Got it."

"We close at two in the morning so make sure you pay

attention to the time. If I have to chase you down and make you leave, you won't be granted membership."

"Two, right."

Riker turns and opens the secondary door, motioning Jack in. Jack rushes through and disappears into the crowd. His eagerness is slightly concerning, and I make a note on his paperwork to review security footage to see how he does tonight. If he doesn't take it down a notch, he's not coming back.

"Was that necessary?" I ask Riker when I finish with my note.

"What?"

"The macho act."

"I told you before, I don't share. If you don't like it, too bad."

I roll my eyes. "I'm not asking you to share, Riker. I'm asking you to trust that I can handle myself."

"Luna, I have zero doubt you can handle yourself. Shit, you've handled yourself against me and I'm no slouch." He kisses my forehead. "But as long as I'm around, I'm going to be protective."

"You mean possessive?" I counter, trying to inject annoyance into my tone and based on his smirk, failing miserably.

"That too."

"Fine," I huff out and turn back to the desk when the front door opens.

I spend the next hour checking in four new potential members. Riker goes back inside the club to keep an eye on things. He's insisted on helping out, acting as a bouncer of sorts and agreeing to that was one of my compromises to get him to stop begging me to cancel tonight.

At midnight, I lock the front door. People can still get out, but no one can get in. We're full enough for a Free for All night, especially when you factor in the regular members who couldn't stay away.

When I walk through the club, I take in the music, the way members are interacting, everything. Riker is at the bar, helping Libs serve drinks, and he smiles when he spots me. I point to the stairwell, and he nods.

I head up to my office. I lock the door at the bottom of the steps because Riker has the code but leave the one at the top open. I cross the room and settle into my chair, kicking my feet up onto my desk. I'm exhausted and let my eyes drift closed, telling myself I'm just going to rest for a second. I'd give anything to be able to sleep, but I can't. Even after we close for the night, Riker and I have to make the rounds to do security checks at all the safe houses.

Just a few minutes of rest, that's all.

"Looney Tunes!"

I startle awake so hard my chair almost tips over. Riker rushes forward and steadies it, laughing at me the entire time.

"What the fuck?" I ask, my voice husky from sleep. "Why would you do that?"

"Do what?"

"Scare me like that."

"I tried to wake you up, but you were out cold. Yelling was my only option."

"I can think of better ways you could have handled that," I mumble.

"Okay, yeah, me too," he admits. "But that was funny."

"I'm glad I could amuse you." I stand up and stretch. "What time is it?"

"Two-thirty," he says and walks to the two-way glass overlooking the club. "We got everyone checked out and the club cleaned up."

I thrust my hands through my hair. "I'm sorry, I didn't mean to fall asleep."

"It's fine, Luna," he assures me. "You were exhausted. I checked on you a few times and decided it was better to let you sleep."

"Well, thank you."

Riker winks. "You can make it up to me later."

"I will. But first, we've got security checks to do."

"Yep," he agrees. "I've been checking in with everyone all night and so far, so good."

I breathe a sigh of relief. The world didn't end because I took a nap. "Okay."

"C'mon. We'll get our rounds done and then you can sleep as long as you want. Jacks and Jills opens later tomorrow and everyone else can handle anything that might come up."

"Sounds like a plan to me."

CHAPTER TWENTY-SEVEN

If there's anyone else still in that house, there's no hope for them.

Riker

"How many houses do you have left?"

I toss my cigarette to the ground and grind it out with my boot before answering Gibson.

"Just the one." I scrub my hands over my face. "Luna's talked to both Spooks and Lashes, and they've assured her that everything is fine, but she still insists on going."

"Do you want me to go check it out? I'm sure you two could crash here for the rest of the night."

"Nah, I'm good."

"Are you?" he counters. "You've been burning the candle at both ends for weeks now. You can't keep this pace up much longer."

"Is that the doctor or brother talking?"

"Both," Gibson says. "Seriously, Riker, find a way to get some rest. If not for yourself, then for her."

He nods toward the house, and I turn to see Luna coming

down the walkway. I can see the exhaustion in the way she walks, hear it in the way she talks, but she refuses to stop. Maybe Gibson has a point.

"Everything good?" I ask when she steps off the curb toward my Harley.

"Yeah. Kenny was having a rough night, so I sat with him until he fell asleep."

"Why was he having a rough night?"

"He said he saw someone outside of his window." Luna waves her hand dismissively. "Normal stuff I think."

"Definitely no one outside his window," Gibson says defensively.

"I know." Lune straddles my bike. "And that's what I told him. That he has a lot of people watching over him and if there were someone outside his window, the person would've been caught. It's fine, Gibson. Promise."

"Well, on to the last house?" I ask, getting on my bike in front of her.

"Yep."

"Gibson, call if you need anything," I tell him before revving the throttle. I settle my hand on Luna's thigh. "Ready?"

"For you, always."

I throw my head back and laugh as I pull onto the road, pointing us in the direction of the northernmost safe house. I navigate the sleepy neighborhood while Luna squeezes my sides between her thighs and rests her cheek against my back. I keep my hand on her, lazily moving my fingers to keep her awake.

The drive seems to take forever, despite there being little to no traffic, and when I pull off the highway on our exit, I relax a little. The streetlights illuminate our way until we hit the outskirts of this little burg and then it's nothing but country roads and open spaces.

When we're a little over a mile away from the house, Luna taps my side and then points toward the sky ahead of us. I follow her hand and my stomach drops.

It's a full moon but even if it weren't, I'd still see the smoke. Flames lick the sky, a bright display of the hell they're creating on solid ground.

I push my Harley as fast as I ever have and the closer we get, the more alarmed I get. Luna's frantic behind me and I have no doubt that she'd throw herself off the bike and run the rest of the way if she thought it would get her there faster.

I turn onto the road the house sits on and the heat becomes suffocating. The house isn't fully engulfed yet, but it won't be much longer before it'll become impossible for anyone other than firefighters to get in and get people out. I park as close as I can without risking our safety, and Luna jumps off. I grab her arm before she can get anywhere.

"Where are you going?" I demand.

She yanks out of my grasp and whirls on me. "I'm going inside. I've gotta get them out!"

"The fuck you are. We're staying right here and calling 911."

"No fucking way."

With that, she turns and takes off. Stubborn woman. I chase after her, dialing 911 as I run. When a dispatcher answers, I shout my emergency into the phone, as well as the address, and hang up. With Luna now inside, I don't have time to answer any questions. Either they can figure out they need to send help, or they can't. That's on them.

I see a busted window at the side of the house and despite the loud, deadly sound of the blaze, I can hear Luna as she calls out to everyone.

"Spooks! Lashes! Barb!" Luna's voice is getting scratchy, no doubt from smoke inhalations. "Paulina!"

I grip the window ledge and jagged shards of broken glass tear at my hands as I lift myself up and through the opening. When I hit the floor inside, just below the window sill, I pull my shirt up over my mouth and nose and frantically look around for Luna.

"Luna!" I shout but I get no response.

I can't tell where anything is because the room has filled with smoke so thick, I can barely see my hand when I lift it directly in front of my eyes.

"Luna, where are you?!"

Sweat pours down my face and creates a salty soot that burns my eyes. I blink rapidly to try to keep my vision clear. I push to my feet and yell for her again.

"Lun—"

"I'm right here."

I hear her before I see her. One foot breaks through the haze, then another. And then two more.

Wait, what?

When Luna's entire body becomes visible, the look on her face and the gun pointed at her head sends cold terror through me, almost as if crystalized frost is rushing over my veins, inch by inch, until my entire body is frozen.

"Riker, I'm—"

"Shut the fuck up!"

Just behind Luna, gun in hand, is Paulina. I recognize the pistol as Luna's and wonder how the girl got it away from her. Not that it matters. She did and now she's dangerous. I reach for my weapon and a fresh wave of panic hits me when I feel nothing in my waistband.

Motherfucker!

Paulina's face is black with soot but there's no mistaking the glint in her eyes. She's loving this. She shoves Luna forward, closer to me, but before they reach me, the ceiling comes crashing down, no longer able to withstand the fire.

I feel Luna's body collide with mine when she tries to dodge the falling debris and a second weight hits us both and sends us tumbling through the window. The wind is knocked out of me when I hit the ground, but I still manage to roll to the side, with Luna in my arms, in an effort to get away from Paulina.

I glance up at the opening and see Paulina standing there, flames behind her, gun pointed at us. I have no idea why she's not jumping but I take advantage of what little time we have to get away.

"C'mon, Luna," I say as I grab her arm and help her to her feet.

I drag her across the yard, both of us coughing violently. Luna struggles to get away from me, yelling about needing to go back, desperate to find the others, but I refuse to budge this time. If there's anyone else still in that house, there's no hope for them.

"Looney Tunes!"

Luna digs in her feet, forcing me to turn with her to look back at the house. Paulina is still standing inside, and the sight is haunting, like some fucked up horror movie.

"I'm sorry!" Paulina shouts and spreads her arms wide.

The fire surrounds her, swallows her up like unforgiving quicksand. Her screams are broken, tortured, and unbearable to hear.

"Oh my God," Luna mumbles beside me. Her hand digs into my arm as she squeezes me like a lifeline.

"I think you mean Lord Luxuria."

Luna and I stiffen before slowly turning around and coming face to face with the monster we've been hunting.

CHAPTER TWENTY-EIGHT

Not all hope is gone.

Luna

"I have to say, I'm a little disappointed you weren't in that house with the others when the fire was set."

I stare at Conrad Templeton with a level of contempt and hatred I've never felt before. I've often wondered what Hell is like or how I would act if I met the Devil because let's face it, with all the things I've done, heaven isn't the obvious option for my afterlife. I guess now I know.

"How did you find this place?" Riker asks.

That's one of the million questions hurling through my mind but haven't been able to ask. My words are stuck in my throat, unable to push past the lump taking up residence and threatening to cut off my airway.

"Are you that stupid?" Templeton counters but the question is rhetorical. "Do you honestly think my daughter ran away? That's ludicrous. Paulina did exactly as she was instructed, and she will be rewarded with many pleasures in her next life, in the Land of Sinfinite Opportunity."

"Where's everyone else who was in the house?"

Templeton shrugs. "I imagine still inside." He takes a few steps toward us. "Now, I'm going to need you to do exactly as I say because I really prefer not to shoot you both."

"You're fucking nuts if you think—"

A gunshot echoes in the air and it's quickly followed by Riker's howl and my scream. Riker falls to the ground, and I drop to my knees next to him. I press my hands to the wound to help control the bleeding, but it doesn't do much good. Riker needs a doctor, fast!

"What did you do that for?!" I yell.

"Oh, he's fine," Templeton says. "It's just his leg. He's not going to die anytime soon."

"I swear to God, if you—"

Templeton pulls the trigger again, cutting off Riker's warning, and this time, the bullet strikes the ground, kicking up dirt and grass.

"I'm not going to tell you again," Templeton snarls. "God doesn't fucking exist in this world. I do!"

Crazy. That's the only way to describe this man. Absolutely, one hundred percent off his fucking rocker.

"What do you want from us?" I ask.

"I want you to pay for your sins." He closes the distance between us and glares. "Get up."

"You shot him in th—"

"I said get the fuck up!" he screams.

I help Riker get to his feet and he sways slightly. He's lost a lot of blood and I'm not sure how much longer he can stay conscious, let alone alive.

"The police and fire department are on their way," Riker says as he leans most of his weight on me for support. "You won't get away with this."

Templeton laughs. "Which is why we're leaving." He steps around us and pushes the gun into my back. "Walk."

He guides us to the garage behind the now fully engulfed house. The door is already open and inside is a truck with its engine already running. How the hell did he get in here? How did he get past Spooks and Lashes? At the thought of my sisters, tears spring to my eyes. There's no time for crying. I can break down later.

One thing I'm grateful for is the fact that there weren't any Soulless Kings stationed at this house because we thought it was the most secure due to its remote location. That was obviously a massive oversight but one I can't be too angry about. Had they been here, that would be more death on my hands.

When we reach the truck, Templeton pulls four zip ties out of his pocket and secures them around my wrists and ankles, as well as Riker's.

"Get in," Templeton barks.

I awkwardly climb into the cab of the truck first and movement in the back catches my eye. I turn to see what it is and am shocked to see Spooks lying on her side with her hands and feet bound. She's got duct tape over her mouth, but her eyes are open.

Riker gets in behind me. His breathing is labored, and his face is pale. When his eyes widen, I know he's seen Spooks. I can't help but wonder where Lashes is but at least not all hope is gone.

"What did you do to her?" I ask Templeton when he gets into the driver's seat.

"I didn't do anything," he says as he turns the key in the ignition. "If I had, she wouldn't be alive. Unfortunately, my daughter still had a little sliver of conscience left and she must have liked her because she didn't give her enough poison to kill her."

"Poison?"

"I can see I'm going to have to spell everything out for your very simple mind," Templeton grumbles. He pulls out of the garage and onto the road, pressing on the accelerator as we head in the opposite direction of where we came. "Yes, poison. It seems I taught my daughter well. The night she *ran away*, I gave her explicit instructions to find the almighty savior." He glances at me and glares. "That's you, in case you're wondering."

"I'm not," I snap.

While Templeton continues, I work on the zip ties around my ankles. They're tight and I'm not sure I can make them budge, but I have to try. It doesn't take long before the plastic cuts through my skin and I feel something wet trickle onto my hands. I push past the pain and keep trying to break free.

"Paulina was always a weird child. Defiant, unruly. Beatings didn't help much but I kept at it. When she reached an age where I could sell her, she begged and pleaded with me not to." Templeton is staring out the window, his expression almost… wistful. He continues as he drives. "Imagine that. Here I had this kid who hated me so much, but the second she was going to be separated from me, she couldn't bear it. So I made a bargain with her. Do what I needed her to do, help me take out Delia McAllister's insane daughter, and she could stay with me."

"Your daughter didn't stand a chance as long as she was under your thumb," Riker says.

"No, she really didn't. But she was too stupid to realize it. And I capitalized on that stupidity and her insane love for me."

As Templeton navigates the curvy roads, I can hear Spooks rolling around in the back, her body banging around in the truck bed like a sack of potatoes.

"I don't get it," I say, more to myself than to him.

"What's there not to get?"

"There are so many places, other businesses you could have chosen. Why Jacks and Jills?"

"There's that simple mind again. Jacks and Jills is full of people who already do questionable things," he says. "And they like it."

"We're not the only BDSM club out there," I argue.

"That's true. But the level of power a lot of your members have is perfect for my needs. The teams that were formed out of Jacks and Jills? They made some of the best annual games we've ever had."

"You are one sick fuck, you know that?" Riker says. "I have no idea how Trinity survived your reign of terror but trust me when I say, no one else will ever have to because your empire will fall."

"No, it won't. I will always overcome."

Silence fills the cab of the truck. Every few minutes, I glance over my shoulder to check on Spooks. It's hard to see her in the dark but every time I look, I can see her struggling to get out of her binds. When I notice that she has her hands free, hope fills my chest. If I can do the same thing, then there will be two of us against one and we'll have the element of surprise.

"Where are you taking us?" I ask, trying to distract Templeton.

"To my kingdom, of course."

CHAPTER TWENTY-NINE

Luna is definitely a keeper.

Riker

My eyes drift closed, and I fight to keep them open. Between the pain and the blood loss, it's getting increasingly difficult to stay awake, but I have to, for Luna. I grip my cell phone in my hand and pray I hit the right speed dial and Fender is hearing everything Templeton is saying.

I have no idea how the maniac missed it, but my phone was in my back pocket and when we got in the truck, I immediately started to work on getting it out. I knew if I could just get someone on the line, we could be tracked.

"Your kingdom?" Luna asks for clarification.

"I'm surprised you haven't figured out where that is yet." Templeton leans around her to look at me briefly. "You too, for that matter. For as much research as has been done by your respective clubs, I kept waiting for you to show up at my door." He straightens and returns to watching the road.

"Don't get me wrong, I'm grateful for your incompetence, but it would have been much easier to handle you on my own turf. Smaller body count."

"H-how much longer until we get there?" I croak.

"Why?"

Before I can answer, Luna rests her head on my shoulder and her hand grabs mine behind our backs. I glance down at her, and she mouths the word 'free'.

"What are you two doing?" Templeton slams on the brakes and throws the truck in park before turning to face us. He grabs Luna's arm and yanks her. "Sit up!"

When he's satisfied, he faces forward and grips the steering wheel. "I don't know why you insist on making this harder than it has to be," he grumbles. He rests his head on his hands. "All you have to do is sit there and be quiet so I can get you to my house and kill you. Is that asking too much?"

"Yeah, it is," Luna snaps. "What about either of us makes you fucking think we're gonna just roll over and die?"

"I should have known Delia's daughter wouldn't go down easy," he mumbles. "Did you know she fought me?" Templeton leans back against his seat and smiles wistfully. "She fought me tooth and nail. Delia didn't want to die. She begged for her life, bargained more than anyone else I've ever killed. It was pathetic."

"Don't you dare talk about my mom," Luna snarls.

"The last words out of her mouth… now those were pitiful," Templeton remarks, ignoring Luna. "'My love'. That's what she said. 'My love'." He quickly glances at Luna and smirks. "I assume she was talking about you." He shifts his gaze to me. "And you. I thought for sure you'd catch me. But Lord Luxuria prevailed."

Templeton puts the truck into gear and starts driving again. "Now, if you'd be so kind as to be quiet, I'd like to listen to some music for the half hour of our trip."

He turns the radio on and spins the dial until classical music flows through the speakers. He cranks the volume, and the instrumental arrangements aggravate my already pounding head.

Out of the corner of my eye, I see Luna's head bob, but she's tapping me from behind and her eyes are open so I can only imagine she's faking it. Finally, her head drops, and she falls against me.

Templeton reaches across to yank her up, but I stop him.

"She's just sleeping," I snap in a harsh whisper, playing along like I'm trying not to wake her up.

He mumbles something unintelligible under his breath but leaves her alone. After a few minutes, Luna presses her head into my chest. I glance down and see her rolling her eyes toward the bed of the truck. I let another few minutes pass so I don't raise suspicion and look over my shoulder as if checking on Spooks.

Spooks is crouched below the window so Templeton can't see her but she's completely free and seems to be planning something. Good. Something has to give.

Just then, a rumbling sound catches my ear, and a sea of headlights crests the hill behind us. I breathe a sigh of relief. No less than fifty bikers are barreling straight for us. I face forward and let my head fall against the seat.

"What the hell?" Templeton grumbles and squints at the rearview mirror as if that will help him see better. He glares at me, his face red with rage. "What did you do?"

"What do you mean?" I ask innocently. "I didn't do—"

The truck swerves out of control and I'm shoved up against the window. We're tossed around in the cab like rag dolls as Templeton tries to regain control and when he finally straightens us out, that's when I realize what happened.

Somehow, Spooks got over the cab of the truck and slid

down the windshield. It must have scared the shit out of Templeton with the way he reacted but miraculously, he couldn't shake her. Her fingers are gripping the edge of the hood and she's hanging on for dear life.

"Stop the fucking truck!" she shouts.

Templeton tries to purposely swerve and dislodge her. He turns on the windshield wipers, does anything he can to get her off the truck. And he fails miserably.

Before I even realize what she's doing, Luna twists so her feet are aimed at Templeton and kicks him as hard as she can. She doesn't let up, kicking him in the side, the face, the arms until he's no longer able to control the vehicle.

I'm still bound, my leg is bleeding but now numb, and thanks to the knock on the head the first time Templeton swerved, I have a nasty gash I can feel oozing. In other words, I'm useless at the moment.

Luna kicks Templeton one last time in the side of the head and he slumps, losing consciousness. She quickly grabs the steering wheel and at the same time, reaches across him to open his door. She pushes him out and scoots into the driver's seat, where she's able to stomp on the brake and bring the truck to a screeching halt.

Spooks flies off the hood and rolls on the ground. The bikers who were behind us are now caught up and one by one, they park and come running to the truck.

"Jesus," Fender mumbles when he opens my door.

"Get this fucking things off me," I demand, shoving my hands in his face.

Fender pulls out a pocket knife and cuts the zip ties. As soon as I'm free, I jump out of the truck, ignoring the shooting pain in my leg as it penetrates the numbness and makes itself known. I hobble around the back of the truck and see a group of Soulless Kings standing in a circle off to the side of the road.

"Is he alive?" I ask as I slowly, angrily make my way to them.

"Yeah," Trainwreck calls over his shoulder. "Barely though."

I glance toward Luna, knowing I need to check on her but unable to stop the rage, and see Mollie helping her out of the truck. Just beyond them is Libs and Pivot, both of whom are kneeling next to Spooks.

"Go help them," I demand of my brothers. "He's mine."

"You heard him," Fender says from behind me.

They disperse and I take the last few steps toward Templeton. When I reach him, I stand there, silent, seething, and trying to imagine the most horrible punishment possible I can inflict.

Pushing past the pain, I haul my leg back and kick him in the ribs. He rolls away from me and coughs violently.

"Get up," I bark. He continues to writhe in pain. "Get the fuck up!"

"Riker, finish him if you're going to but we're gonna be swarmed with cops soon so you need to fucking hurry."

I'm dimly aware of Fender's words, of him clapping me on the back, but my focus is so fine-tuned on Templeton, it barely registers.

"You won't kill me." Templeton rolls again, this time toward me. His face is full of bloody road rash and he's grinning. "You can't kill me. Otherwise, who's gonna take care of your bitch when you're in prison?"

I stomp him in the chest with a booted foot. He coughs up blood and vomit, all of it dribbling down his cheek. He tries to lever himself onto his knees but falls over.

"Riker!"

I whip my head to the side and see Luna coming toward me, a scowl on her face.

"What?"

"Sirens." She points past me, and I glance in that direction. "Don't you hear them?"

I do now.

Fender and the other bikers scramble to their Harley's. He and Mollie stay with Luna and I while everyone else takes off.

"Here they come," Templeton singsongs from the ground.

With each passing second, the sirens get louder and when the cars come up over the same hill I saw the bike's crest before all hell broke loose, I see the swirl of red and blue lights.

"You got lucky," I tell Templeton. "But that luck will run out. I will find you and I will fucking end you. That's a promise."

"Let's go!" Fender shouts.

I hop on his bike behind him. Normally I'd argue but even I know I'm in no condition to drive. And I sure as shit am not getting on the back of a chick's bike. Luna climbs on behind Mollie, but her eyes stay on Templeton.

"You won't find me!" Templeton shouts. "You've never been able—"

Bang.

Bang.

Bang.

Bang.

Luna pulls the trigger in rapid-fire succession and Templeton slouches to the ground, four fresh holes in his body. She hands the gun to Mollie, who tucks it in her waistband and then takes off down the road.

"Definitely a keeper," Fender comments before following them.

As I hang onto my brother so I don't fall off, my lips tilt into a grin. Fender's right. Luna is definitely a keeper.

CHAPTER THIRTY

Wanna see if we can grow some wings and fly away together?

Luna

"Luna McAllister."

I jump up from my chair in the hospital waiting room and rush toward the nurse calling my name.

"How is she?" I ask.

"She's fine. And she's asking for you so if you'll follow me…"

The nurse walks me through a set of double doors and down a long hallway before stopping at the last room on the left.

"You can go in," she tells me. "But please, keep it short. She needs her rest."

I take a deep breath and push the door open. Tears flood my eyes when I see Lashes, her skin pale and almost blending in with the white sheets on the hospital bed.

"Hey," she croaks.

I rush forward and practically throw myself on her to give her a hug. Lashes arms come around me and she squeezes me tight.

"I'm fine, Looney Tunes," she says, a teasing quality to her words. "Just a little poison, some smoke inhalation, and a concussion."

I sniffle as I straighten and then wipe my cheeks dry. "I am so sorry I wasn't there."

"Why? This isn't your fault, you know that, right? You can't protect everyone from everything. We all knew danger came with the territory when we were patched in so quit beating yourself up."

"I just… I don't understand how this happened." I take a deep breath. "Paulina was his victim. Why would she help him?"

Lashes smiles sadly. "She may have been his victim, but he was still her dad. Kids just want to be loved by their parents, regardless of how awful they are."

When she looks past me, I know she's picturing her own childhood. She was severely abused by both parents and up until the age of eighteen, she did anything and everything they asked of her because she wanted them to love her. She showed up at DHMC with a lengthy juvenile record and a boulder-sized chip on her shoulder because of it.

"I thought you were dead," I comment, changing the subject. "Templeton said you were still in the house."

"We would have been, but I think Paulina got the poison dose wrong. I woke up in the basement. And the other girls were tied up next to me. I don't think she had the heart to kill them outright, so she was going to let the fire do it for her. Fortunately, Barb was able to get out of her binds and between the two of us, we got the girls out one of those little basement windows and we climbed out after them."

"Thank God."

"I can't believe no one told you we were okay."

"They might have, to be honest. When we got here, they checked me over and released me. Smoke inhalation is the worst of the damage, but they gave me a valium to calm me down because I wouldn't sit still. My brain is a little fuzzy so… yeah, they may have." I take a deep breath, which sends me into a coughing fit. When it settles, I continue. "Riker and Spooks are in surgery."

Lashes eyes light up. "Spooks is alive?"

"Yep." I chuckle. "She's too fucking stubborn to die."

"What a nightmare," she mumbles.

The door to her room opens and the nurse comes in. "I think it's time she get some rest. Your husband is being taken to recovery so you should be able to see him in a few minutes.'

"Husband?" Lashes asks when the nurse steps back into the hall.

"I had to tell them something. They weren't going to keep me updated on Riker's progress if I didn't." I shrug. "So yeah, husband."

"The word 'husband' rolls off your tongue pretty easily."

"It does, doesn't it."

Lashes grabs my hand. "Luna, I'm glad you found someone to make you happy. Not to mention someone who can put up with your particular brand of crazy."

"Me too, Lashes. Me too."

I leave Lashes' room and search for the nurse so she can take me to Riker's room. I find her at the nurse's station, filling out paperwork.

"Any news on my friend, the woman that the bikers brought in?"

"You mean Ms. Spooks?"

They can't seriously believe that's her real name.

"Yeah."

"She's still in surgery. I'll take you to your husband and then see if I can get an update."

"Thank you. I'd appreciate that."

"No problem."

I follow her to the other end of the hall and stop in front of yet another door.

"He's still coming out of sedation so he may be a bit groggy," she says when she opens in and enters ahead of me. "A titanium rod was placed in his leg due to the damage caused by the bullet. He'll be on crutches for a while and he won't be able to go joyriding any time soon, but he'll be okay."

"Thank you."

"You're welcome." She checks his vitals before walking back to the door. "I'll go get that update for you and give you two a few minutes."

I nod and when she closes the door behind her, I stand frozen in place.

"Come here," Riker whispers roughly from his bed.

I close the distance between us and reach for his hand, careful not to hit his IV.

"Are you okay?" he asks me.

I nod and a tear spills down my cheek.

"Then why are you crying?" I shrug. "Not really digging this whole silent thing. I like it better when you give me a hard time."

I playfully swat his shoulder causing him to wince and groan in pain.

"I'm so sorry," I say, feeling horrible.

Riker chuckles but it comes out more wheezy than normal. "Luna, I was just messing with you. Got you to talk though."

"You're impossible," I accuse.

"Yet here you are, still in love with me."

I grin. "Yep."

"I love you too."

"Oh, guess what?"

"What?"

"Lashes and everyone else who was in that safe house got out. They're all going to be fine."

"Seriously?"

"Uh huh."

"What about Spooks?"

"She's still in surgery but I imagine she'll be on the mend soon."

"Good. that's really good."

"Riker, I am so sorry I got you into all this," I rush to say. "When I started trying to get revenge for my mom, I had no idea the twists and turns my life would take. And I hate that you and the Soulless Kings got sucked into it. I'm so—"

"Luna, stop," he snaps as he narrows his gaze at me. "I've told you before, you don't apologize to me." Riker lifts my hand to his lips and kisses my palm. "I am so fucking proud of how you handled this and beyond lucky that you took me along for the ride."

"How is any of this lucky?"

"Any second I get with you has to be the result of luck. No way do you love me for my good looks and charm." He's teasing me and I love it.

"Still, it's sort of been a shitshow from day one."

"Maybe." He shrugs. "But as long as we're in the shitshow together, I'm happy."

"Ya know," I begin. "My mom told me once that true love is like jumping off a cliff and praying the other person will jump with you so you can fly away together."

"Okay," he says, confused.

"Wanna see if we can grow some wings and fly away together?"

Riker grins.

"I will fly with you anywhere, my love."

EPILOGUE

Death, sir. My safe word is death.

Riker
Six months later...

I park my bike under the Jacks and Jills sign near the road and climb off. It feels odd to be riding again but the doctor gave me the all-clear this afternoon and the first thing I did was drive for a few hours down the coast and back. I wanted to take Luna with me, but she's been busy setting up for a private party at the club tonight.

She's always busy though, especially lately. Having to set up all new safe houses took a lot of time, energy, not to mention money. But she did it and I'm proud of her. Two of the houses are empty right now but that's okay. At least she'll have them ready as more victims show up. Because let's face it, more will come. They always do.

I walk across the lot and when I shove my key into the lock, it doesn't turn.

What the hell?

I lift my fist to bang on the door, but Mollie's voice stops me.

"Please swipe your ID, sir."

My ID? I haven't needed that in months.

"C'mon, Mol. You and I both know I don't need one."

Or maybe she doesn't. Spooks is normally covering the door but since she transferred to another chapter, Mollie's been filling in until Spooks is replaced. Luna was devastated to see Spooks go, but in the end, she recognized that a fresh start is exactly what her sister needed after the night with Templeton.

"I'm afraid without an ID, you won't be permitted to enter."

Annoyed at whatever game she's playing, I grab my wallet and dig out the old photo ID and swipe it on the panel next to the door. Instead of the normal green light, it flashes red and beeps twice. I try to swipe it again but get the same thing.

"Sir, maybe try the correct ID?"

"What?" I snap. "I only have the—"

"Check your wallet again, sir," she instructs. "Perhaps behind your driver's license."

I roll my eyes but do as she says and sure enough, behind my almost expired driver's license is a new Jacks and Jills ID badge. I pull it out and my heart skips a beat when I read it.

Dominic Young
Co-Owner and Platinum Dominant

I swipe the card and the light turns green just as the lock disengages and the door swings open. Mollie stands there with a giant grin on her face.

"Welcome."

"What the hell is going on?" I ask. "Where's Luna?"

"If you'll follow me, please…"

Mollie opens the secondary door and disappears inside. It's dark and I can't help but wonder why. This is shaping up to be a very weird night.

I step through the doorway and am plunged into lights and shouts.

"Surprise!"

The main floor of Jacks and Jills is filled to capacity with Devil's Handmaidens and Soulless Kings, as well as some well-respected and trusted members of the BDSM club.

Luna runs up to me and launches herself in my arms. I catch her easily. A few weeks ago, I'd have wobbled and fallen on my ass.

"Are you surprised?" she asks.

"Um, yeah." I set her on her feet. "What is all this?"

"Well…" She looks over her shoulder and waves for Fender. He hands her a manilla envelope, which she then hands to me. "Here. This is for you. You don't have to read it now, but it basically signs over fifty percent of Jacks and Jills and makes you a co-owner."

"But, why?"

"Riker, brother, this is where you belong," Fender says. "You come alive on the days you know you'll be here. And on the days you should be at Infinite Motors, you're always skipping out."

I hang my head. "Fuck, man, I'm sorry."

"No, don't be sorry," he says and turns to Luna. "Maybe you could explain this better."

I look at Luna and wait for her to explain. She opens her mouth several times, but it takes a few minutes before words come out.

"A few weeks ago, I approached Fender with an idea. President to President." She rests her palms on my chest. "I want Devil's Handmaidens to partner with Soulless Kings for any matters relating to human trafficking. We may have taken out Templeton but as you know, we still have a long way to go to completely wipe out The Church of Sinfinite Opportunity."

"Okay, I'm on board with that," I tell her. "But you didn't have to make me co-owner of Jacks and Jills."

"I know I didn't."

Luna turns back to the crowd, all of whom are hanging on to her every word, and nods at Mollie. Mollie steps forward and hands me another envelope and returns to her spot.

"Open it," Luna says.

I run my finger under the flap and pull out the contents. My eyes focus on the black and white image until it starts to blur. I lift my head and when a tear rolls down my cheek, I realize the photo was blurring because I'm crying.

"Are you serious?" I ask, choked up.

Luna nods and flattens her hands on her stomach. "She's due in six months."

"She?"

"Well, I'm hoping it's a girl," Luna admits. "I'm not sure I can handle a boy with a combination of both our personalities."

I wrap my arms around her to lift her off her feet and spin her around. We both laugh and our friends and family clap and cheer.

"The way I see it," Luna begins when I set her down. "We're going to be flying together for the rest of our lives, at least as parents. Why not fly together in every single aspect of our lives?"

"Luna McAllister, are you asking me to marry you?"

"Fuck no."

Her face hardens and my stomach drops. How did I misjudge that? I take several deep breaths and try to figure out how to dig myself out of this hole and before I can come up with something, Luna throws her head back and laughs.

"Riker, I'm not asking you to marry me. I'm telling you, as someone who outranks you, that you need to ask me." She shrugs. "If you want to, that is."

I grin. "Do you remember your safe word?"

Luna's face reddens from embarrassment, but I don't care.

"Of course I do."

I grip her chin and force her to look at me.

"Excuse me?"

Luna licks her lips. "Of course I do, sir."

"That's better. Now, please tell everyone what your safe word is," I command.

"Death, sir. My safe word is death."

I lean forward and press my lips to her ear. "I will spend the rest of my life taking you to the brink of your safe word," I growl for only her to hear.

I straighten and give everyone else what they want.

"Luna, I will love you until death do us part."

NEXT IN THE SOULLESS KINGS MC SERIES

Trainwreck...

I don't like to talk about my past or my family's history. It's depressing and an unwelcome reminder of the monsters who walk among us, but the people responsible for my family's destruction keep popping back up.

I'm now in a position to do something about it. I have the Soulless Kings MC at my side and, like me, they won't simply roll over and ignore what's happening. When my sister returned, I vowed to take down anyone connected to her disappearance, and I'm making progress. But, like a cockroach, more keep crawling out of the woodwork and forcing me to remain entrenched in their filth. That's why, when the sister of one of our own comes up missing, I take it upon myself to save her or die trying.

Sylvia...

I grew up in the Black Savages MC, but it was my sister who was treated like their princess. I wish I could say I wasn't jealous, but the fact of the matter is, I was. And then all hell broke loose. Right was left and left was right… nothing made sense. My sister married into another MC and I was left alone to pick up the pieces.

I tried like hell to do just that and while I found some sense of normalcy, the pieces never quite fit. One tragedy after another follows me, knocks me on my ass until I simply can't stand back up without help. And when he shows up to play savior, I have no choice but to trust he can get the job done. I also don't seem to have a choice when my heart decides to jump into the mix and confuse everything.

ABOUT THE AUTHOR

Andi Rhodes is an author whose passion is creating romance from chaos in all her books! She writes MC (motorcycle club) romance with a generous helping of suspense and doesn't shy away from the more difficult topics. Her books can be triggering for some so consider yourself warned. Andi also ensures each book ends with the couple getting their HEA! Most importantly, Andi is living her real life HEA with her husband and their boxers.

For access to release info, updates, and exclusive content, be sure to sign up for Andi's newsletter at andirhodes.com.

ALSO BY ANDI RHODES

Broken Rebel Brotherhood

Broken Souls

Broken Innocence

Broken Boundaries

Broken Rebel Brotherhood: Complete Series Box set

Broken Rebel Brotherhood: Next Generation

Broken Hearts

Broken Wings

Broken Mind

Bastards and Badges

Stark Revenge

Slade's Fall

Jett's Guard

Soulless Kings MC

Fender

Joker

Piston

Greaser

Riker

Trainwreck

Squirrel

Gibson

Satan's Legacy MC

Snow's Angel

Toga's Demons

Magic's Torment

Printed in Great Britain
by Amazon